# THE TRAVELLING
# APPLE

Published under licence by Brown Dog Books and
The Self-Publishing Partnership Ltd, 10b Greenway Farm, Bath Rd, Wick, nr.
Bath BS30 5RL, UK

www.selfpublishingpartnership.co.uk

ISBN printed book: 978-1-83952-828-6
ISBN e-book: 978-1-83952-829-3

Cover design by Andrew Prescott
Internal design by Andrew Easton

Printed and bound in the UK

This book is printed on FSC® certified paper

MIX
Paper | Supporting
responsible forestry
FSC
www.fsc.org    FSC® C013604

# THE TRAVELLING
# APPLE

## TALES THROUGH THE JOURNEY OF LIFE

# VIDA CODY

BROWN
DOG
BOOKS

Also by Vida Cody:

*Shorts*
*Baker's Dozen*

*For Mum, Dad and Tia*
*My three best friends*

# CONTENTS

# THE SHELL

It was an old house, derelict now and sad. Windows broken here and there in quietly rotting wooden surrounds, worn through from years of neglect and the lashing of storms against their façade as the wind raced in from the sea.

The house stood lonely, atop the hill, staring out at the horizon from sad empty hollows, scanning the far distance as if waiting for someone to return. Rain rolled down its cheeks, like tears flowing from persistently flooded eyes.

Isolated, inside and out, it stood on its own in the vast expanse, fighting to withstand all that was thrown at it, but slowly being beaten down, frame by frame, joint by joint, its skin torn apart like the ragged seams of a tunic once loved but now discarded.

In the darkening sky, the shutters fell, as if the house had blinked, not wanting to see. It would take some strength to open them, to make them want to look again, to come alive with fresh new hope.

The garden gate had come unhinged, at the fierce battering it took from the squalls, increasingly savage as time went on. Its wooden bars had come apart and lay like the ribs of a shipwrecked vessel, struggling to hold themselves together, aching and moaning in painful display.

Around the gate, fallen trees, once proud, tall and mighty, struck down in a moment of weakness, one by one like a tumbling wooden clown, its antics seen by no one. A debris of timber, leaves and glass, spread out on the ground in disarray, as if an explosion had thrown it there, to lie in tatters across the path, awaiting perhaps a craftsman's hand, to piece them together in a modern mosaic.

Inside, the house was desolate, an empty shell coiled in on itself. No light appeared within its walls, save for that from the broken panes which cast an intermittent glare, throwing shadows in eerie forms. Its curtains swayed upon the draught that seeped through every nook and cranny, swirling at intervals in a *danse macabre*, guiding an unseen partner around, oblivious to the lack of applause and moving in time to an unknown beat.

Voices, carried on the wind, rose and fell like the waves of the sea, echoes from a distant past. Shrill and pleading, like the cry of a bird that sought safe haven from the maritime storms, having travelled for weeks and months to arrive, in the hope of finding its former mate and settling down to raise a family.

The décor drab and faded now, no welcome sight for man or beast, a poor reflection of its glorious past, the rooms once full of light and happiness. The paintings taken from the walls, leaving a dull and dirty stain, marked with age and grim abuse. Candle wax upon the floor, soft and smooth still to the touch. A table laid for a party of twelve, its plates crawled over by resident mice, looking for any scraps of food to fill their hungry bellies.

A creak on the stairs and a human step, cautiously treading by the light of a torch which swept ahead in a nervous arc. Into the hall the girl came, scanning the room's every corner, looking for what, she hardly knew, though she recognised all that was there before her.

She remembered setting the table out, carefully placing the cutlery, arranging the glasses and champagne flutes, the napkin rings and finger bowls. The centrepiece, a maple leaf triton, lovingly carried home from Taiwan, still lay flat with its wings spread out, tarnished now and less of a beauty, though calling her yet from its clouded horn.

The shell, like the house, spoke to her and made her feel at one with them. Empty the three, devoid of love, of hope, of dreams, of happiness. Tossed back and forth on the waves of life, no son of Poseidon watched over them now, but let them drift on a restless sea that swallowed them up in its cavernous mouth.

Stripped of the softness that once lay within, all that remained was the outer casing, its colour diminished with the passing of time. Gone were the life, the joy and the laughter, each having folded in on itself.

While the scars of the shell and the house were visible,

for the girl the pain was deep inside, like winter had come and put down its roots, twisting around her very being, trapping her in its strong embrace, encasing her in its tangled twine. Her days, like the roots, had been strung together, indistinguishable, one from another, stretching out in front of her like a long road without a horizon.

The girl hunched within her coat, as she looked at the dinner party before her, empty and silent in a friendless house. No easy chatter sounded there, no popping of corks, no chinking of glass. No calls for a dance when the dinner was done, no scraping of chairs in readiness.

She took up the shell from its place on the table and gently held it to her ear. She wanted to hear what it had to say, to listen for echoes of the past, to wait for the wisdom it might impart. But all she could hear were the sounds of the sea as it scraped over the shingle beach.

She knew that none of them would return, that every one was lost to her now, gone for good in this cruel world. Like faces drawn upon a page, all together they'd been rubbed out, with little trace of where they'd been, not even a footprint on the sand.

Days went by in a howling wind, in rains that beat upon the house as it watched over an anxious sea. A traveller happened upon the scene, and hoping to find some refuge there, hammered hard upon the door. As it gave way, the man stumbled into the dark, his hand searching for any possible switch. Thunder rumbled overhead and a bolt of lightning ripped across the room, long enough for him to see the remains of a large shell crushed upon the floor and the body of a girl hanging above.

# ON HUNGERFORD BRIDGE

Half past five, on Hungerford Bridge. I am swimming against the tide, as some would say I've done all my life. Going against the flow, as I have since childhood and throughout my teenage years, marching on into adulthood, always against the crowd, much as I am doing now, fighting my way against a wave of commuters, head down and resolute on their journey home.

My father was just like me (or I like him), I am told, for I never knew him, his having died when I was a wee bairn, living then in the Scottish Highlands. We shared the same name – Donald McDonald – as fathers and sons often did in those days. I soon changed that, of course, one of my first acts of conscious rebellion that was to become my stock in trade.

I'd been seen to revolt long before that, refusing to conform even as a toddler, unwilling to sit quietly and do my painting or join in the games with the other boys. 'An unsociable lad,' my school report said, 'he needs to mix and make some friends.' Such bluntness has followed me all of my life, doggedly marking my every step, right on my heels with its scathing judgements, always trying to trip me up.

I wasn't unsociable and wasn't a loner. I knew what I liked and knew what I didn't and resented those who told me otherwise. To each his own, I've always said, and my own is mine alone. Nobody else knows me best, whatever they all might say, and some, it is true, have said a great deal.

Being told what to do is tiresome and carries a heavy weight. Why be burdened with such instruction when you know your mind yourself? I've known *my* mind from an early age and what is wrong with that? Plenty, others would frequently say, as they tried to change my direction. But I set myself on a definite course and wouldn't deviate.

At school, I had never fitted in, bored with the classes and bored with the teachers, tired of learning dates and formulae, conjugated verbs and the subjunctive clause. I hated structure and time ill used and longed for a different type of life. I was neither academic nor practical and certainly never into sports. Kicking a ball around a pitch or batting it over a three-foot net was something the others were left to enjoy, for I was having none of it. Back and forth that ball would go in what seemed a pointless exercise. That others could enjoy such games was a constant source of amazement to me, but each to his own, as I've said before.

I never did well in my school exams, though I could have done if I'd applied myself. My family and teachers despaired of me and were always saying to pull up my socks, but I wanted to leave them where they were, stuffed in a drawer in the family home – metaphorically as well as physically.

I'd never been a tidy kid and never liked a uniform. I had to wear it, of course I did, or else I'd have been expelled. School was very strict in those days and my parents would have been horrified if little Donald had been chucked out. I never would have minded myself, though doubtless they'd have sent me somewhere else. I always made sure my shirt hung out and my tie was half undone. And never, never would I wear that cap or I'd look like Billy Bunter.

As soon as I had come of age I was up and out of town, eschewing the paths that others took in joining the family firm or heading to university. Neither route appealed to me as I wanted to plough my own furrow, not sit in one that was ready made.

I took a couple of gap years long before they'd become the norm. Off I set, on my own two feet, an adventurer and a wanderer traversing the globe from west to east, taking the odd job in between in order to fund my travels. I never stayed in a place too long as I didn't want to look established or seem like I had settled. The nomadic life suited me. It was all I really wanted.

I started off in Germany – Frankfurt, Bonn, Stuttgart and Munich – then travelled by train through Austria and on from there to Budapest, cut in two by the River Danube, with hilly Buda and flat Pest and very impressive architecture!

# The Travelling Apple

On further east to Romania, then south and across to Istanbul, one foot in Europe, the other in Asia. I loved the energy of the Grand Bazaar, the hustle and bustle of myriad traders and those who sought a bargain there. In and out of the souks I went, haggling here, haggling there, while marvelling at the textiles and jewels and wondering how I'd carry them home. I bought myself a small rug, rich in hues of orange and red, and knew I could find a space for it wherever I ended up throwing my hat.

I flew from there much further east, on the long journey to Tokyo, arriving in the *sakura* season. How beautiful the cherry blossoms, their soft pinks caressing my soul, as I strolled beneath them in a cloudless sky. Families and friends seated below, tucking into their bento boxes and sharing a bottle of rice wine. Happiness carried on the air, from the laughter of couples enjoying themselves. Salarymen, away from their desks, amused at the giggles of girlfriends and wives, relaxing on a warm spring day and comforted by the delicate blooms.

That night, by contrast, I sat at the ring, enthralled by the grandiose sight before me of two heavyweights in loin cloths battling it out in a wrestling match. Tough buttocks on tough sumo men hitting the ground with considerable force. The dull sound remains with me still as I think of those heady nights on the town, reminiscent of rhinos fighting for dominance, their skin thick and their power great.

# The Travelling Apple

The Silk Road beckoned me next and along its length I journeyed home, its ancient empires filling my mind. I chose to follow the southern route, a single way through the Karakoram Mountains, as opposed to the more northerly route that split in three as it wended its way.

Seeing myself as Marco Polo, I set off on my expedition, travelling south from Lanzhou, across the People's Republic of China. I made my way to the Karakoram, struggling badly to communicate and wishing I'd shown more interest at school. If I'd paid more attention to other tongues, I might be more inclined now to tackle one of the hardest languages and at least be able to ask for food rather than point at it helplessly.

Riding a camel was new to me but appealed to my innate sense of adventure. It added, I thought, a touch of romance as we plodded along in our camel train. I was Lawrence of Arabia now, though still too far east to be truly authentic. How beautiful my dromedary looked, with his long eyelashes and bushy brows. I envied his long, powerful legs, as I myself was rather short and hadn't the balance the camel had, despite having more toes than him. Big, wide feet splayed out beneath me, keeping us upright as we progressed, surely and silently, on our trek.

Huge dunes of red and yellow, like pictures I'd seen in my history books but more alive than on the page, stretching as far as the eye could see. Buddhist caves and wooden temples, historical forts and ancient ruins, greeted us along the route, as we journeyed on through Central Asia, our transport varying as we went.

On through the Hindu Kush, mountains I'd only dreamt about, with their snow-capped peaks and breathtaking views, holy sites and terraced fields. I thought of the people who had passed this way, trading merchandise and knowledge; of the populations who'd come before me and the mix of cultures, ideas and beliefs. I thought of the silks and their origins, of the fibre produced by the silkworm's cocoon, of its high value and renowned prestige. How blessed I was, to be here now, walking in old and sacred footprints.

My journey, I knew, was edging towards its end and soon I must return home. I worked my way through Afghanistan and Turkmenistan, mainly helping out in backbreaking jobs on the land or washing up for long hours in hotel kitchens. Anything to earn some more money and allow me to move steadily west.

Finally, on to Iraq and Baghdad, my last stop before flying home. Once the largest city in the world, Baghdad was of major cultural significance until its importance slowly began to decline after the Mongol conquest of 1258. It took until many centuries later for it to regain prominence as the capital of Iraq.

Back in London, it all seemed a dream, as I wandered the streets aimlessly, washing up on Hungerford Bridge. The trains clattered along at my side, their carriages creaking as they entered the station, at the end of their journey, just like me. I leant on the bridge, looking down at the river, watching the tide on its way downstream.

I looked across to the Festival Hall, built as part of the Festival of Britain, helping to raise the nation's spirits after years of austerity and rationing. But standing here now, having just come home, I could see no reason to celebrate. I stared at the swell of people before me, a tsunami of faces heading my way, its force threatening to overwhelm me. I felt the drag of its undercurrents, as I fought to maintain my own pace.

Was this the life I wanted now? Tied to my desk from nine to five? Moving en masse with hundreds of others, grey men in grey suits, walking in the same direction, year after year after year after year?

My recent travels a beacon of light, I fought my way against the tide. A nomad I had started out, a nomad I'd remain. I headed back to London Heathrow and a plane that would take me away.

# A SUITCASE FULL OF PHOTOS

Black and white, black and white, black and white, colour. Black and white, black and white, black and white, pause. Maggie was sifting through photos again. Who *were* these people? If *she* didn't know, no one would. The pile of unrecognisable faces was getting bigger, threatening to topple onto the floor.

Cracked with age and faded, torn at the edges and crumpled up, after years of handling and then neglect. Her children had shown no interest in them, had never wanted to know who they were. Why, she could never understand. They *were* family, after all, or so she assumed.

Some had clearly been taken in studios, the stiff formal pose a giveaway. Upright men with straight backs, standing behind the women, seated in heavy crinolines. The occasional child in a sailor suit, shoes nicely polished and hair neatly brushed. Faces that stared from an ancient page, unseeing now they were long since gone.

The battered old case was full of them, itself a relic from a distant past. Once on its way to a seaside resort, now the keeper of silent memories.

# The Travelling Apple

Maggie had to make a decision before her children made it for her. Secretly wanting to close the lid and keep its people safe inside, she bent instead and gathered them up. Don't look back, she told herself, as she placed the photos on the funeral pyre. Lighting the match, she muttered a prayer: ashes to ashes…

# PLEASE JOIN THE QUEUE

Gerry remembered her first time well. She was eighteen, with money in her pocket and glamour in her head, and on her way to her favourite shop. She'd never yet set foot in the door but had stood outside many a time, looking in at the beautiful clothes, artfully arranged on the mannequins.

It was the shop on the high street that everyone knew, a few steps along from the Catholic Church and comfortable in its own setting. It boasted those large, almost frameless windows, that allowed the light to penetrate, revealing the gorgeous clothes inside.

Gerry had often stood and looked, like countless other local women, admiring the dresses and skirts within, the tailored jackets and boleros. The latest fashions were displayed in that shop, each season something new, attracting many a female eye. The goods were truly coveted, especially by those who had no money, which was most of the women roundabouts. But it didn't stop them having a look and dreaming of what might, one day, be.

The lady who ran the shop was Ann, a friendly soul and very petite. She could have modelled all of the clothes and would have looked great in all of them, but she didn't so much as try them on, trusting instead in her own style. In truth, it was said that she could have worn rags and still would have looked quite beautiful, for Ann was refinement personified, from her coiffured hair to her size three feet.

The highlight of Ann's (and her customers') year was when the January sale came round. She dressed the windows exceptionally, arranging the garments carefully. As much as possible went on display, to show the range of the stock she had, but without it looking far too crammed or detracting from its elegance.

She had an eye for what would sell, what was in vogue and what was a fad. She knew her customers intimately and the style of dress that was right for them. They, in turn, just idolised her and trusted everything she said. No one left the shop unhappy and that, to Ann, was success indeed.

Excitement was building in the town, as Ann opened the doors on the sale. The queue was stretching down the street, as it had for many years past. Prices were dropped considerably, so that others who couldn't normally afford it, were able to pick up a bargain or two. One of those was Gerry Reid, who had joined the queue with her friend Joleen. Neither had been in a queue before and hadn't known what to expect, but it was all very orderly, with a lively and happy atmosphere. They chatted to others in the queue, newbies like the girls themselves and veterans from yesteryear.

When they finally reached the door itself, the two girls were at fever pitch. Ann showed them round the shop, inviting them to try on the clothes and helping them see what would suit them best. Gerry left with a full-length coat while Joleen went for a stylish jacket, both enraptured by their purchases.

That was their first experience of queueing, but by no means destined to be their last. Nor would it be so disciplined when next they came to join a queue.

They were soon in line for a pop concert. They weren't really known as gigs back then and certainly not when it came to the Osmonds. Alan, Merrill, Wayne, Jay, Donny and last but not least little Jimmy. The girls already had their tickets but had to queue nonetheless. Hundreds of screaming Osmond fans filled every street in the vicinity. Though the stewards tried to keep them in line, it was something of a hopeless cause as they were far outnumbered by the girls.

The noise went up in decibels when the Osmonds appeared in their sequined jackets. 'Crazy Horses' sent them all wild as those at the front tried to rush the stage and the show was halted temporarily. Donny was sent to calm them down and plead to the girls to return to their seats, but that gorgeous figure standing there, only had the adverse effect, as the girls swooned before his feet.

Later that night, when the show was over, and the stewards were left to the detritus, Gerry and Joleen joined the throng that had all but totally obscured the bus stop. A crush of teenagers hanging about, all singing the Osmonds' songs, some of them more in tune than others but all in a perfectly joyful state.

But where was the queue for the 205? Were they in the right place at all? It was hard to see the stop itself, as they found themselves in a rugby scrum, pushed back and forth by the hookers and props, being used as a human battering ram. A far cry from the queue at Ann's, professional almost and civilised.

It wasn't the queue they'd been led to believe was part of the British way of life. Part of the nation's DNA, inherited from our ancestors. It was something that others admired us for, the respectful way we all lined up, often in silence, patiently. Thank goodness they couldn't see the girls now, caught in a rough and frightening mêlée.

When the bus came, it was much the same, pushing and shoving, trying to board. It was difficult even to stay together or not be knocked clean off their feet. They should have walked part of the way and caught the bus a few stops down, but it was too late to think of that now. Joleen tripped getting on and Gerry nearly fell over her. They were lucky indeed that neither was hurt as other girls pushed on from behind.

The following day, the two of them met, to talk about the night before and their first time at a pop concert. They had to queue at their local chippy, as the fish was always cooked to order and thus was very popular. A young man tried to push in but the girls were learning to stand their ground and moved their way on up the line.

An old school friend was a trainee there and managed to bag them a few more chips and an extra pickled onion or two. But he didn't have his eye on the ball and nor did the man who was training him, as the fish was badly undercooked, as Gerry's tummy would testify.

Joleen grabbed her mobile phone and rang the doctor's surgery. 'You are number eighteen in the queue', a cold and disinterested voice announced. 'Please hold the line', it said, 'your call is very important to us'. After half an hour of hanging on and waiting to become number two, Joleen heard she was number twelve before the speaker cut her off. Twice more this happened to her, before she finally gave up. If she listened again to the same announcements and the adverts for laxatives in between, she was sure she would throw a hissy fit. A few hours later, Gerry was fine and began to hatch a plan.

What if the two should *start* a queue, rather than constantly be in line? Imagine, to be at the head of it, with everyone else filing behind. Being the ones to lead for a change, not the ones to follow. In pole position, there at the front, waiting for the green flag to go up. Not at the end, not in the middle, but at the very head of the queue.

Two days later, they took themselves off, seeking their spot with utmost care. They chose the Tower of London, no less, arriving at 8 am. Plenty of time to ready themselves and take up their chosen space.

None of the crowds had yet arrived, in the cool morning air. They watched as the beefeaters wandered by, resplendent in their black and red. They gave them a cheery little wave and the Yeoman Warders smiled and waved back.

How proud of themselves the two friends were, as the queue started to form. Out of nowhere they seemed to come, happily falling into line. Just in ones and twos at first and then in their regiments. Whole armies of people, marching with good intent behind the girls, in a straight line, in ready obedience.

A beefeater quietly watched, amused at the sight of it all. He ambled over to let them know they were queueing in the wrong place! He pointed out a big, wooden sign that showed where the real spot should be. Guiding them all over en masse, 'Please join the queue,' he said.

# HAS BEANS

It had never seemed right somehow, to be eating baked beans in a cemetery. At home, yes, in a greasy spoon, yes, but not amongst the graves and the flowers. It was all wrong. Disrespectful even. Yet here she was, sat at the table, dressed all in black, enjoying her beans. White bread, for they didn't taste the same on brown, and a nice hot cup of tea.

It made sense really, if you thought about it. Some mourners travelled a long way to be here and it was good to have somewhere to go if you arrived early. Rather than sit in the car or stamp your feet in the crisp winter air, watching the conveyor belt of corteges slide by, a cosy warm cafe was just the ticket. Coffee with a little snifter would always go down well, especially when fighting the cold, and more so when fighting the blues. But beans on toast? Here in the cemetery? Was it right?

The priest sitting opposite didn't seem to mind, as he tucked into a steaming lamb stew. He seemed, indeed, to be relishing the moment, completely oblivious to his sombre surroundings and licking his spoon with obvious delight.

My God, he'd be licking the bowl soon. Was he here to officiate? Or was this one of his regular haunts? A handy place to pop in for lunch before going home to write his sermon.

Sylvie sat and looked around her. Nothing here seemed right at all. The proprietress laughing on the phone, the Hobnobs and Pringles on the counter, even the pictures on the walls - of children playing in the sea, a load of brightly coloured balloons and a vase of Van Gogh's sunflowers. Maybe meant to make you happy, cheer you up on a sad, grey day, but she wasn't convinced that it cut the mustard.

Sylvie, in fact, wasn't sure why she was here at all, even if the beans *were* tasty. She hadn't come far, just up the road, so could have eaten her beans at home rather than here with the undertakers. Yet here she was, with the funeral set, waiting for another hearse to arrive. Alive or dead, it was always the same – Paul, her ex, was always late.

As she wiped the remains of the sauce with her crust, Sylvie thought back to her countless boyfriends, all still living as far as she knew, all except Paul, who she'd never missed since the day he left her for another woman. Sylvie wondered if *she'd* be here or if he'd dumped her too and moved on. He wasn't what you'd call a 'stayer', leaving a trail of women behind him from the moment he'd turned fourteen.

Other men she wished she'd kept, if she hadn't been playing the field herself. The delectable John and dishy

Derek, to name but two of her roll of honour. They might be here too, as they'd both known Paul, and she squirmed at the thought of them all lined up, a band of has-beens from a former life.

The priest stood up and cleared his throat, pushed back his chair and went outside as the suite of cars he was waiting for, moved slowly towards the little chapel. Sylvie swallowed her last mouthful and followed him out into the cold, the crumbs from her toast left on the plate, much like the beans of a glorious past.

# THE YEAR OF THE DRAGON

My name is George, but my friends all call me Georgie, as if I'm a little boy still, not the man I became, not the giant of legend. They say I'm too big for my boots, that my story has gone to my head, so they tease me and pull my leg, to keep my feet on the ground. But my feet are in the stirrups, astride my noble steed, as they were when my story began, in a country you now call Turkey.

Many countries revere me, as they have throughout the ages, from back in the eleventh century, in what we knew as Cappadocia, when I first came to prominence. Word of me soon spread and my story became well known, celebrated from the east to the west for my honour, courage and strength. The people of Silene, in Libya, hailed me as a hero when I came to save their town. A dragon that dwelt in their midst, was frightening the local community, as poison spewed from its mouth, threatening to harm them all. They began to feed it sheep, in the hope it would go away, but still the beast kept coming, roaming the countryside. Humans were fed to it next – men, the children and young – till it turned to the king's daughter, when I appeared on the scene.

Stood as a bride at the lake, as the dragon emerged from the water, the princess was ready to die and tried to send me away. I charged the dragon on horseback, wounding it with my lance, making it roar in pain. But I wasn't ready to kill it and led the creature away, on the end of my lady's girdle, like a dog upon its leash.

The people were still afraid, so I made a deal with them. They must put their faith in Christ and agree to be converted, then I would kill the dragon and the town would be at peace.

I don't remember the year, for my narrative's passed through time. For me, it was the year of the dragon, for I've never met one since.

Stories about me abound and my name is venerated. The Crusaders called me their own, an early red cross knight, but others say I was Roman, an officer in the army. My story has pre-Christian roots but not attributed to me, and history became mixed with folklore as I passed slowly down through the ages, the symbolic representative of good over evil.

I even became a Saint, dying for my Christian faith, with feast days celebrated all around Europe and as far away as Africa. I share my day with Shakespeare, who honoured me in his play.

Somehow, I've come to be English, though I never set foot on your soil. Like St Patrick who wasn't Irish but is always claimed as their own.

# The Travelling Apple

I don't mind that my friends still tease me, tear me down a strip or two, but I don't like the nationalist cause and the symbol I've been made to become. Should the dragon rise again, I'll be ready with my lance.

# ITADAKIMASU[1]

Cathy felt unhappy again. She often felt like that these days. In fact, there was hardly a day when she didn't feel like that. Two long years she had been like this. Two very long years. Ever since Peter had died and left her on her own. Not his fault, of course, but all the same, it had had a huge impact on her life.

She'd always thought of herself as a strong person. Never one to panic or make a fuss. Cathy was very calm, very placid and nothing had ever fazed her, not even Pete's death really, not at the time at least. Friends had shuffled round her, some not knowing what to say, others trying to take command, but Cathy had wanted none of it and had much preferred to sort it all out herself. It wasn't like she was incapable. In fact, she was quite the opposite and busied herself straightaway, arranging the funeral and dealing with the paperwork. It was all done with her usual, quiet efficiency. All done and dusted before anyone had even realised.

It had been a shock, of course, Pete's dying like that,

---

1   Japanese for 'To humbly receive', said before a meal to show gratitude and respect.

and worse as she'd not been there. Graham had broken the news on a long-distance call from Japan. Graham, her husband's best friend, who was with him at the time and had witnessed his last moments.

They'd been on a business trip, on the island of Honshu, exchanging ideas and knowledge in the field of aerospace. Japan was well known for this, especially in R&D[2], and the men had learnt much on their visit, the second in less than a year. They'd formed some useful contacts, a network of clever men and the token female scientist waving the sisterhood's flag. The trip had followed the usual pattern of working hard all day and playing hard all night, especially on their last night in Tokyo when there was no work to get up for the following day and their flight didn't leave until three.

They'd gone with their Japanese colleagues to a karaoke night. Pete wasn't normally a singer but went along with the crowd, on the basis that anything he sang, wouldn't sound out of tune if warbled in a different language. His counterparts' English might be good but it didn't extend to knowing whether 'Bubbling Brown Sugar' was in key or not. As Graham had said, if Jagger can sing it, so can you!

The evening had not been too unpleasant and, truth be told, they'd found it good fun. Their colleagues loved to let their hair down and were wholly bent on enjoying

2   Research and Development

themselves. In a strange way, it was somehow contagious, and it wasn't long before Pete took the floor, mike in hand and strutting his stuff, to a rousing rendition of 'I Want to Break Free'. He received such tumultuous applause that he went on to sing another of Queen's many hits: 'Another One Bites the Dust', his impression of Freddie Mercury set at once to become a legend.

Had the evening ended there, Pete would have come home safely and Cathy would not be a widow. The group had gone on to dine that night, in a colleague's home in the Shinjuku district. Graham and Pete felt truly honoured and were looking forward to Reiko's cooking. The only woman in the department, Reiko was not just a highly respected scientist, but was also renowned for her expertise in the kitchen and was always proud of her Japanese cuisine.

She knew she should not have let her husband help, particularly where the *fugu* was concerned, even though she'd kept what she thought was a very close eye on him. Reiko herself had cooked it before, to utter perfection and great acclaim. It was a brave person indeed who would have attempted it, without the long and careful training, but Reiko was meticulous in her work, in the department and at home.

The fish itself was beautifully laid out, its delicate flesh nicely arranged in thinly sliced segments. A popular delicacy in Japan, but famous for its lethal toxin, which could kill a human with less than a milligram. Within no time at all, Pete's lips had gone numb and he'd quickly suffered paralysis. Unable to breathe, he had died on the spot, to the stunned horror of those around him.

Reiko had naturally been distraught, going over and over again in her head how the fish had been prepared. She was sure she'd cut out the lethal parts but a miniscule amount must have remained. Unable to come to terms with it, she took her own life in a matter of days, depriving the world of an eminent scientist and a most beloved friend.

It had been left to Graham to break the news, to Pete's young widow sitting at home. Despite the shock and disbelief, Cathy had booked herself a flight and prepared to bring the body home. Those who knew her were not surprised at her action and practicality. This, they knew, was Cathy all over, even when faced with her husband's death.

Her cool, calm nature backfired on her though, as friends assumed she could always cope. Two years on, she knew she couldn't, not without Peter by her side. Life elsewhere carried on as usual, almost as if nothing had happened. People, it seemed, were quick to forget the horror of that late night meal, Pete's death and Reiko's suicide. It was all as if it had never happened, though the truth, for Cathy, was all too real.

She put on a brave face, of course, for she wouldn't have known how to be any different. Not so much the stiff upper lip, but a distinct trait hardwired within her. Whenever anyone asked how she was, she always gave the standard response, the reply she was naturally expected to give: 'Yes, I'm fine thanks, how are you?' It was, after all, what they wanted her to say. Had she said any different, they wouldn't have heard, or wouldn't have listened, more to the point. No one heard the pain in her voice or saw her eyes cry out for help, for this was Cathy and Cathy could cope.

It seemed to them, she was always busy, always out and about with friends. Her life was filled with meaning and purpose, or that is what they'd come to assume, and Cathy did not disillusion them. She'd never lied or made things up, just went about her daily life, trying to fill it with something to do. She wasn't ever enjoying herself, just using the hours till she went to bed, and those hours to Cathy were long.

She'd been a few years older than Pete, her toyboy as her friends had said, but that had never mattered till now. Cathy had retired early, when the shop she was working in went bust, but Pete had been good for a few years yet and in any case just loved his job. Cathy had never really enjoyed hers, though she liked the camaraderie when out with the girls on the shop floor. She never saw them any more. They'd all somehow faded away, to other jobs or their families.

She'd thought to get another job but couldn't face the thought of it now. Too much stress wasn't good for you and the world of work, to her, had changed. Everything seemed too serious now, everyone keen to climb a ladder, pushing and shoving to reach the top with little regard for how they got there or who they chose to trample on. This had never been Cathy's style and she knew she'd no longer fit in.

But where, she wondered, did she fit? She looked at the young office girls, in their high heels and smart suits, mobile and coffee, one in each hand, as they hurried along to work. She looked at the families in the park, enjoying a summer's afternoon; at the courting couples, hand in hand, blind to all but themselves. Nobody noticed the solitary figure eating her sandwich on a park bench, feeling the cold of the world around her.

Cathy longed to have someone to talk to, share a joke, make her laugh. It was far too long since she'd had a hug or felt the warmth of a human touch. She felt as though she were in a bubble, looking out through clouded eyes, not a part of the life around her, which carried on its merry way, unseeing what was in its midst.

Cathy had always had lots of friends but they rarely seemed available. Some still worked and were pushed for time, playing catch-up at weekends, with household chores and with family. Cathy had never had kids of her own, had never been the maternal type, but she wished to God that she had them now, to give her some joy and company. She wondered should she buy a dog, to join her on walks, play ball together, but still she craved a human voice, someone to share a pot of tea.

Cathy knew she must make an effort and really start

to plan ahead, rather than act spontaneously, to better her chances of company. For she was tired of long days and of reaching the evening unable to remember what she'd done in the morning, as it seemed so long ago. Busy doing nothing but dragging herself round the streets, in the hope of finding a purpose in life.

Her friends all thought she had a wonderful life, out all the time, never at home. Those that worked were even jealous, that she could go where she liked and do as she pleased. But doing it on her own wasn't fun, not when it was every day. She sighed each morning at the day ahead, wondering how she'd fill those hours, what she'd do, where she'd go. It was a struggle now to leave the house, with no purpose in doing so, but every day she forced herself out, in an attempt at having a change of scene. She went to places she'd always loved when she and Pete had gone together, but they had lost their meaning now and were even, dare she say it, boring.

She'd thought about having a holiday, but there again she'd be on her own. There'd be others on a tour, of course, but Cathy had lost the way to converse and in any case had nothing to say.

Her friends hadn't noticed her giving up, having assumed she was out enjoying herself. How they'd have loved to jump in the car, drive to the beach or countryside, but full-time work hindered this. Oh, how lucky Cathy was, to be a free woman without any ties.

She always seemed happy whenever they met, but they didn't realise the reason for this. A couple of hours of company was more than she'd come to expect in a week. No wonder she looked so overjoyed!

And now, they'd learnt, she'd enrolled on a course – not just one, but three in fact! They wished so much that *they* had the time, instead of being tied to a desk, and – for many – tied to the home as well. Yes, how lucky Cathy was, never a care in the world.

Cathy had indeed enrolled, as a way of making new friends. She deliberately chose from the daytime classes, as the evening courses were for those who worked. She'd opted for pottery, plumbing and French and intended to stick to all three, a mixture, she thought, of fun and usefulness. At least one, with any hope, might lead on to something else and, if very lucky, to a new man in her life. She still missed Pete very much, of course, but Pete would not want her to be unhappy and would wish her to find love again.

Gradually, over the next few weeks, amidst the coils, the casts and the chucks, Cathy and Stuart became quite attached, which was more than could be said for their pots. They often met at the red-hot kiln, waiting to see their latest disaster and urging each other to try again.

Stuart finally plucked up courage to ask Cathy out for a meal. He knew a nice little restaurant, he said, where the food was lovingly and beautifully prepared. On the night, he chose the food for them both, from a menu all in Japanese. The fish was a real delicacy, he said, as the waiter placed the *fugu* before them. Now, tell me about yourself, he said.

# THE NIGHTHAWKS

It was a Thursday evening on the lower east side. Nobody who was anybody should have been out on a night like that. A cold wind blew the length of the street, its long tongue licking round every building, winkling into every nook and cranny. The storekeepers had closed their doors, turned off the lights and hidden away, for these silent streets aren't safe at night and only the mad will walk their darkness.

Those of sound mind were locked at home, sitting by the bars of an electric fire, aglow in its heat, not out on these streets. The blinds were half down at Tony's place but nobody stirred in the rooms upstairs and were no doubt huddled in the room out the back.

The only light for me that night shone from the window of Phillies' diner, though there was little cheer and little warmth even in that most hallowed den. Mickey McGraw sure kept his place nice, its counters wiped clean of coffee stains, its floors polished and free of filth. But the light that shone out to the lonely streets was a beacon waiting to be extinguished.

Sonny was sat with his latest broad, the red-haired dame from the music hall. Bambi was the name he called her, for her very large and expressive eyes, though the similarity ended there. For one look at you could kill a man dead, like the sharp blade of her stiletto heels.

Smokey the Gaol-Bird was in that night, having lately left his gang inside. They'd rubbed out the Six some years ago but Smokey had managed to gain parole and now sought refuge at Phillies' again.

But one of the Six had not been dead and had bided his time till his moment came. For no one gets one over on me, no one wounds the great Rowley Brown and lives to tell the tale.

Content to hide in the shadows that night, I waited until they'd said their goodbyes. I followed Smokey down the street, his burning cigar blinking away, revealing his whereabouts up ahead. My soft suede shoes gained on him till we reached the dock and I pushed him in. Then I made my way back to Phillies', another light having been put out, and ordered a brandy and soda.

# FOR MILA, WITH THANKS

I guess it had all started with Mila, the little toddler who stole my heart. She wasn't mine, more's the pity, but the daughter of my best friend Max and his lovely wife, Doroteia.

Max and I were at school together and later at university, he reading Portuguese and I studying dentistry. He had a flair for languages and spoke at least five, I know, but Portuguese was his real passion from a very early age.

He said he had fallen for Carmen Miranda and it had all gone from there. Carmen Miranda. The singer and dancer who brought us the samba and sent my friend quite literally bananas! The Brazilian Bombshell with fruit on her head and rhythm in her toes. Max, like others, had been enchanted by her and had determined to learn her language. He'd never mastered her dancing skills and certainly couldn't sing, as his gurgling attempts in the shower testified.

Max had met his wife by chance, in a port cellar in the Douro Valley. He'd taken a summer vacation job, helping out in one of the caves, serving the wines and ports to tourists. He seemed to her so knowledgeable, so full of life and passionate, while she – to him – looked just like Carmen, minus the obligatory bowl of fruit.

The two at first had just been friends but before too long they were inseparable and within a year became engaged. I, of course, was Max' best man, though I struggled with my wedding speech. I might be good at filling teeth but was no good when it came to tongues. That I left to my linguist friend, who fluently praised his wife and me. Or so I believe.

They honeymooned in Estremadura, the Portuguese Riviera and the peninsulas of Lisbon and Setúbal. They visited vineyards and olive groves and dined in traditional fishing towns. They sat on the beach at Peniche and learnt to surf on the Atlantic swell.

Two weeks quickly went, and now they were married, it was time to decide where they would go to put down their roots. I was very glad when the decision was made, to come back home to the UK, although home for Doroteia had always been Portugal. It hadn't been an easy choice but one that they made completely together. I confess I was afraid of losing Max and knew it would never be the same again, but at least he'd be back on home soil and we could still meet up from time to time.

In fact, they went out of their way to include me, to make me one of their family. I hadn't lost Max, I had gained Doroteia, as the couple embraced me with open arms. We were often seen out together, enjoying meals and evenings out, but it made me wish there was someone for me, someone special, of my very own. In a strange way it made me lonely as I said goodbye to the pair at night. They went off in each other's arms while I went home to an empty house.

I threw myself into my work, frequently clocking up extra hours or covering for colleagues who were sick or on leave. I loved my job and the rewards it gave, in knowing I'd cared for somebody's teeth. So many patients asked for me, as I always tried to put them at ease and help them to overcome their fear.

I liked to help the children best when they came in looking terrified. The waiting room I filled with toys, with colouring books and Lego sets, to take their mind off rotten teeth and the thought of what their dentist might do. I gave them gifts for being brave – cuddly bears and little jigsaws, pencil sets and simple games, items I'd bought from a charity shop that looked like new and did the trick. I loved to see the smile on their face as they left the practice with clean, healthy teeth and a new toy to take home. For me, it made it all worthwhile.

Max, meanwhile, was in academia, teaching his beloved Portuguese and working all the hours God gave. He was also carrying out research, on his favourite poet, Luís de Camões. Little before was known about him and Max set out to put this right, documenting the facts he could and planning to travel to Portugal to further his investigations there. His dream was to follow the sea route to India, described in Camões' epic poem that told of the famous navigator, Vasco da Gama, and his voyage out east.

His dream, however, was put on hold, when Doroteia announced she was pregnant. Max was the perfect dad to be, fitting in work around his wife and arranging his teaching accordingly. There was nothing he wouldn't do for her, his charming and charismatic wife.

A beautiful girl was born to them early in the summer months, after complications and a long labour. They immediately decided to call her Mila, their own little miracle. Dark haired with large eyes, they knew – when grown – she would break a few hearts and gain a throng of admirers, very much like her mother had done.

I myself was captivated by the small bundle of pure joy who gazed at me so constantly, as if she was trying to communicate. Genuine love drained from those eyes, in that innocent little baby face. I'd never seen anyone quite so perfect as Mila was to me back then.

But perfection, it seemed, could surpass itself and she steadily grew even dearer to me, as she outshone herself as a toddler. Watching that little girl playing, happily chortling and running about, steps uneven and arms outstretched, I couldn't help but be enchanted at the sheer joy and wonder of it all.

Perhaps it was time to settle down, to stop playing

gooseberry. Doroteia and Max had been kind to me and were still more than happy to include me, though I knew they'd love to see me married, with a wife and children of my own. Perhaps, deep down, I wanted that too and it had taken Mila to show that to me.

I started to go out more on my own, joining clubs and ramblers' groups and events that had always attracted me. But the women always seemed attached and so I continued to go it alone.

I carried on as I'd done before, working hard at my dentistry, available always to those in need. I also resumed my visits to Max, not only for the company but to share in his wonderful family.

I doted on young Mila still and she, in turn, was fond of me. Her eyes lit up when I entered the room and she rushed to hug me round the knees. I sometimes thought that she'd never let go, her arms tight around my legs, her head resting on top of them.

Many times I would babysit while Doroteia and Max went out, allowing them a romantic meal or a night down at the picture house. One such night, when Mila was in bed, the doorbell rang quite suddenly. I wasn't expecting anyone but went to see who the caller might be.

There before me, in radiant beauty, a Carmen Miranda lookalike! I thought at first I was seeing things, that my mind was playing tricks on me. She looked, indeed, like Doroteia, standing there smiling at me. I blinked and slowly rubbed my eyes, till a soft voice spoke to me. This heavenly vision was actually real, though ethereal still she seemed to me.

Her accent then gave her away, before she'd told me who she was. This was Doroteia's sister, come – she said – to babysit, though it was now approaching nine o'clock. As little Mila was fast asleep, I poured Calista a glass of wine and we chatted easily into the night.

When Doroteia and Max returned, I – like Mila – was fast asleep, the effects of drinking too much wine. Doroteia was most amused and joked that her sister had bored me to sleep on what would become our first date.

The evening had been planned of course, by best friend Max and his lovely wife. They'd sought a mate for my lonely heart and found her in the gorgeous Calista, younger sister of Doroteia. Not your standard blind date but one that worked famously, to the happiness of all concerned.

Our relationship quickly blossomed and I knew that I had found 'the one'. Not that there'd been many others, but I knew deep down within my heart that Calista would be my bride. She, in turn, seemed to idolise me, though why she did, was anyone's guess. Max had said that she liked my smile and the fact that my teeth were always clean!

We married in Lisbon the following May, on the banks of the River Tagus. The city was bursting with colourful flowers, their scent carried on the warm spring air. Max of course was best man and had taught me some words for my wedding speech, though whether I really carried it off remains a mystery to me. I had seemed to raise a few laughs, but whether at my simple jokes or my desperate attempts at Portuguese, I guess we will never know.

Little Mila was bridesmaid and took her job seriously, as she followed her auntie up the aisle. Once or twice she stood on her train but quickly shuffled back a step and hoped that nobody noticed her. Carrying a small posy of flowers that matched a circlet on her head, she looked herself like a mini bride, radiant on her wedding day. Little Mila, my favourite child, with me as I took my vows, giving her biggest and brightest smile. If not for her, I wouldn't be here, I whispered to my darling bride.

# THE BEARSKIN

Hannah loved looking at photos. The older the better, in black and white or faded sepia. Individuals from long ago, in formal dress and formal pose, staring out of a crumpled mount, asking to be brought alive again. Each one flat upon the page, waiting for the kiss of life and the breath that would wake them from their sleep. Real-life characters in their day, with names and personalities, with families and places of work, be it office, home or factory. People going about their day, just as Hannah was doing now, as she emptied the box onto the floor.

She was meant to be clearing a cupboard of junk, in the hope of creating a bit of space for her collection of Ordnance Survey maps. She would love to house them all together, in proper alphabetical order, rather than leave them to their fate, haphazardly scattered in every room.

A battered box had caught her eye and halted the sifting of *objects d'art*. Once the lid was cast aside, a glorious treasure became revealed – a horde of family photographs. Pretty girls in fancy frocks, little men in sailor suits. Women standing, hands on hips, moustachioed husbands by their side.

Hannah's eyes met the gaze of a handsome man in uniform. A soldier in the Coldstream Guards, smartly dressed in his red ceremonials, tunic brushed and buttons gleaming. His face had a knowing look about it, sad and aged before its time, though he couldn't have been but one and twenty. Deep were the eyes that looked at her and called her from that seasoned face.

His bearskin proud upon his head, a fine sword hung at his side, this guardsman spoke of bravery, of battles won and battles lost.

Hannah rifled through the photos, hoping he would appear again, perhaps as a boy or an older man, or with a bride on his wedding day. She scanned the faces of family groups, of individuals, couples and friends, but all she found were other men, in suits and ties and civvy street.

Until, that was, he came again, but this time there was something different – the bearskin on his head was missing. Hannah searched back through the pile, to find the original photograph, but though she looked at every one, it simply seemed to have disappeared. The one in her hand was almost exact, save that it showed a bare head. The handsome face remained the same and seemed just now to be smiling at her.

Hannah put the photos away and placed the box back in the cupboard. Later that night, when she went to her room, she stopped and stared in front of her – the missing bearskin was on her bed.

# KITTY MALONE LIKES FOOD

Kitty Malone was on a diet. Again. Kitty Malone was always on a diet. Some said that she had a weight problem, but that wasn't strictly true, for Kitty just ate too much.

She'd always been the same, had Kitty, even as a baby. Born a healthy 8lbs 2oz, she fed like a wolf on her mother's milk and never seemed to be satisfied. Her little mouth would clamp on, sucking for all her life was worth. A wonder she was never sick but Kitty Malone held on to her food till passing it out the other end. She certainly looked a bonny baby, full of verve and vitality, with lovely, big, rosy cheeks like a hamster storing its cache of food.

She kept that look as a toddler, adding to it those chubby legs, so endeared of girls that age. They should have given her some support, strong and sturdy as they were, but Kitty couldn't keep her balance and regularly ended up on the floor. Every time she tried to stand, her little body toppled forth and she looked like a tortoise righting itself, having landed upside down on its back.

When she finally managed to take a few steps, she could only waddle rather than walk, but it got her where she wanted to go, albeit clumsily. She'd have been better off with webbed feet, to give her a better and even balance.

At primary school, she sat at her desk, chair pushed back to allow for her belly, on which she rested her thick little hands. Nobody really took any notice, as long as she was comfortable. Her skirt had an elasticated waist, which became the norm in later life, allowing her to breathe more freely and not to feel so hemmed in.

While her playmates detested the school meals, Kitty always shovelled it in, going up for seconds or thirds and eating the food from others' plates. She had a voracious appetite and didn't like to see food wasted, even at that tender age. 'There are children starving in Africa', the nuns had said at every lunch, 'they'd be very glad of your daytime meal.' Kitty took them at their word, feeling sad for those with nowt and appreciating every bite. She felt she'd be letting those children down if she didn't consume what was on the plate, food they'd relish if given the chance. Best not to make it worse.

At secondary school she was much the same, though by then she often took a packed lunch. Two rounds of sandwiches, a pork pie and a packet of crisps – family size to keep her going through double maths in the afternoon. An apple was also always consumed, not because she wanted it – Golden Delicious was not her bag – but because she felt she was cleaning her teeth and keeping the doctor and dentist at bay.

Kitty was friends with everyone, not least for her stash of lunchtime food, which she'd trade for a bun or a chocolate bar if others' tuck was more appealing. She was first in the queue at the school shop, jingling her coins in her money belt and eyeing up all the goodies on offer. She longed to run the shop one day, to have first dibs on the new stock, but for now that job was out of reach and she had to content herself and wait.

Kitty Malone was great fun. She had a certain zest for life and threw herself into every day. She was very much a thoughtful girl, taking care of those in need and always appearing first on the scene whenever anyone cried for help. She could always be relied upon to give up her seat on the local bus or carry the shopping for those who struggled. Kitty had an inner peace and knew who she was from an early age. She never let anything get her down and overcame all obstacles by shrugging and simply carrying on. Her attitude was a God-given gift that others less fortunate could only admire and wish that their make-up was just the same.

As Kitty grew up, her weight increased. For some she was cuddly, for others rotund, but Kitty just tried to be herself. She knew she enjoyed her food too much but that was her passion and interest. She ached to be a chef one day, experimenting with different foods and maybe running a restaurant. She might have to go abroad to train, but Kitty was more than happy with that. Imagine, all the different foods, all the different tastes to savour.

Her imagination was running riot as she flicked through her cookery books. Colour plates of sumptuous food, mouth-watering recipes. She couldn't wait to devise her own, plan some meals and entertain. Hard work could make it happen, so Kitty began to apply herself.

She started by cooking food for friends, simple dishes that were easy to prepare. Often one-pot cookery, to avoid a lot of washing up. Her friends were most appreciative and regularly came to Kitty's house, ready to sample her culinary delights. They joked that she'd one day poison them if they spoke out of turn about her food, but Kitty wasn't the killer type and took it all with a pinch of salt.

Kitty applied for an apprenticeship after gaining good grades in her A-levels: maths, biology and chemistry, to help her with her chosen path. She excelled at understanding the science and its implications for cooking food. She knew there was more than the practical side if she wanted to become a professional chef.

The apprenticeship was challenging, with long hours and much to learn, but Kitty was more than up to the task and soaked up the atmosphere like a sponge. She found she was able to work under pressure, to keep her cool and carry on, while others around her were struggling.

Soon she became a *chef de partie*, working in a small restaurant kitchen, preparing the food for the lunchtime rush. She chopped the vegetables, meat and fish, daily improving her knife skills and wielding the blade with great aplomb. Julienne cuts and chiffonade, dicing, mincing and batonnet became her regular stock in trade. Never once did she cut herself, though she knew she'd often come too close.

A dab hand at plating food, Kitty arranged it all like a painting. Her presentation was a work of art, a visual feast for her customers, that kept them coming time and again. She knew how to draw the foodies in and the restaurant's takings went through the roof. Even a basic salad dish looked appetising and beautiful, its contrasting colours an artistry that stimulated the taste buds.

There were few who saw her behind the scenes, working away at her chosen craft. An inspiration for those who did, Kitty appeared a natural as she went about her wizardry. She seemed to work effortlessly with an in-built creativity, but that disguised the hours of work and sheer hard graft and industry.

Kitty's reputation grew as she worked her way up the hierarchy. She sourced her ingredients locally and was keen on seasonality, supporting her farming community and keeping her menus fresh and new. Her imagination simply flowed as she rummaged around for ingredients, devising flamboyant and novel creations for her growing legion of gastronomy fans.

Kitty Malone was larger than life, with her high spirits and *joie de vivre*. As popular as she'd always been, for her character and her culinary skills, Kitty was always surrounded by friends. She had a certain presence about her, lit up a room with her infectious smile and dazzled just by being there. The very epitome of fun, her body shook and quivered with mirth, as she melted into the atmosphere, the toast of all her colleagues and friends.

By nature of the job she had, Kitty continued to put on weight. She had, of course, to sample her food, to taste her various recipes, before offering them up to anyone else. This was never a hardship at all, for Kitty, we know, just loved her food. She also found she was snacking too much, grabbing whatever meals she could, in between her numerous tasks.

Her health began to deteriorate, with high blood pressure and cholesterol. She then became prediabetic, heading for some serious risks. Lifestyle changes had to be made, to keep the blood sugars under control. Working with nutrition experts, Kitty set out to lose some weight, on special diets first of all, then trying to eat more healthily. Though this was not an easy task, the pounds began to fall away, revealing a new slimline self.

But how could Kitty keep this up, with her love for food and her gourmet ways? She soon slipped back into dangerous habits, on a path that risked her health again. Back on the diet Kitty went, on a rollercoaster of ups and downs.

Many wondered how she would manage, with such an insatiable appetite. She literally was a glutton for trouble and would surely never cope. But this, for Kitty, was a new challenge and one she determined to meet head on.

Using her culinary expertise, she began to prepare new recipes. Sourcing the best and freshest ingredients, she aimed to reduce the fat she ate. She found she could still eat tasty food and make delicious and exciting meals. She managed to stave off the hunger pangs and satisfy her appetite by filling up on a range of veg, with protein and high-fibre carbs that still looked a picture on the plate.

Always a keen and natural swimmer, she began to take more exercise. Down at the pool five times a week, up and down Kitty went, increasing the number of lengths she swam. Her friends were all in awe of her, though not surprised at her drive to succeed. Would she survive her new regime or fall back on her wolfish ways? Of course she'd survive, of course she would, for this was Kitty Malone.

# FROM WOMB TO TOMB

No one could quite remember when it was first conceived. It was like it had always been there. Quietly growing, behind the scenes, until ready to burst forth in all its ugliness. A seed that would germinate, grow new shoots and turn into a monster so repellent that even she would scarcely recognise it. Her own offspring. Once out, it could never go back, but then again, she'd do nothing to try and stop it.

No one knew how the seed had been planted or what had caused it to grow at all. It was like it fed on its own body, tearing chunks from its own flesh, gnawing away at every sinew and savouring every bite. It wasn't a pleasant feeling to have, this *thing* growing inside you, not for most women anyway. But for Cassie Jonquil, it was her pride and joy.

She would regularly stand at her garden gate and chat to any passers-by, rubbing her hand over her belly, softly cooing to the form within. Encouraging noises, spurring it on, telling it how she was on its side. Every so often, she'd feel it kick, reminding her it was still there, and lovingly she would start to caress it, this creature of hers, growing inside.

# The Travelling Apple

For nine months she carried it, feeling it move and start to develop. Her eyes gleamed as she thought of it there and a smile would ease across her face. She knew what she wanted this *thing* to become and knew how she would help it there. Cassie would do all in her power to help this being on its way. No holds barred, she would not stand back but create a path that was free of stones. Nothing would stop its sure progression, no one would stop its steady growth.

No one had seen this creature coming, not until it was far too late. Safely hidden in Cassie's tummy, it lay beneath layers of maternity clothes. Until such time it was more than a bump, more than a swelling or protuberance. She carried it with a certain panache, with a showy swagger and confidence. This brute was hers and she'd nurture it, tender it till fully grown.

Came the day when the beast was born and Cassie was in her element. Keeping her newborn close to her, she cradled it in her arms. It suckled on its mother's milk with a voracious appetite. Its cheeks went in and out like bellows as it pumped away at her swollen breast, its hideous head lolling from side to side as it did so. All who saw it thought it ugly, a monstrous Caliban, half animal, half human. People turned and looked away and never met its gaze. Its roar could be heard throughout the land, sonorous and repetitive like a knell announcing the dead.

As time went by, it grew and grew, becoming ever more malignant, eating away at Cassie's soul with its usual rapacious force. Yet still she fed and strengthened it, still she urged it on. Cassie held it in her arms, swaying gently back and forth. This cold-blooded issue from her body, this reptile of epic proportions.

Resentment and anger its middle names, it sought to vent its spleen. It actively looked to cause distress as it made its way on its harsh and relentless mission. It never let up but hardened itself as it slowly chased its quarry down, stalking its prey with the stealth of a fox, patience a misguided virtue.

Superiority seeped from its veins as it looked down its long, scaly nose. It sought out those who would pander to it, feed its ego, confirm its worth. Its disordered mind wanted attention and someone new to admire it. It saw no incentive to understand or care for the feelings of others, holding fast to their past mistakes like a barnacle stuck to a ship.

It cared not at all what happened to them, what damage it might have caused. It only cared that it took command and displayed its imperious self. It consumed the hand of the one who'd fed it, devouring then her every limb, finally coming to overwhelm her and gobble her up both body and soul.

Throughout its life she'd carried it, keeping it close to her very heart, moulding it into its hideous shape, unleashing it when provoked. In time, the beast would self-destruct as its nature backfired on itself. Exploding with centrifugal force, it ripped itself apart in a flash. Now its innards were fully exposed, its name engraved in their midst. The abomination that for many years had taken Cass over and dominated her thinking, was finally laid bare for all to see. Cass had been carrying a grudge.

# A VERY DIFFERENT BEAST

Miss King was a force to be reckoned with. Something of a tyrant in office circles, who regularly reduced her colleagues to tears; a bully, who thought too much of herself and too little of others and who wasn't afraid to show it. Indeed, she thought it a kind of glory when girls were found weeping in the ladies' toilets, the result of a scathing and withering look or a harsh and caustic word meted out, often in the presence of other colleagues – always, if she could possibly manage it, to let them know the power she had.

She was, for certain, a dominatrix, someone you'd try to avoid if you could, and management (unfortunately) did just that. She seemed to wield an authority, though in truth she was only a minor player, way down the list in the hierarchy. Miss King had worked there some forty years and showed no wish for her looming retirement, planning instead to carry on, waving her flag of dubious standards. Staff these days were lacking in sense and education, at least in the mind of the mighty one who saw it her duty to sort them out, to bring them to heel, to subjugate.

She swooped with glee at a new recruit, sinking her

teeth into juvenile flesh, licking her lips with undisguised relish as her victim fell in front of her, waiting to take whatever came. And come it did, each one going the way of the others, torn to pieces by the office vulture.

Many colleagues had up and left, unable or unwilling to become her prey, getting out while the going was good, which usually meant just a matter of days. No one knew how to handle her or approach her in her solitary lair, the only one with a room of her own, that overlooked the atrium and commanded views of the terrified staff as they tried to escape her constant gaze.

She stalked the floors like a lioness, stealthily moving in search of the weak, sniffing them out in their covered hides, then pouncing upon them with snarling teeth. Safety in numbers didn't exist, as she scattered the herd in a single stride, isolating the vulnerable while preparing to launch a new attack.

How she'd remained in post for so long was a question that legions of colleagues had asked. She hadn't ever progressed through the ranks and had never particularly wanted to, for she already had complete control and money was of little interest to her.

Miss King came from wealthy stock, having inherited a vast fortune from her excessively rich father, a businessman of some repute before an unfortunate incident on a longed-for safari with a young rhino in heat. Much had been said in the papers at the time, but over the years it became old news and Miss King herself never mentioned it.

In fact, no one knew anything about her private life or what she did when she left at night. She was simply Miss King, harridan of the office, scourge of the people, a permanent fixture that nobody wanted but couldn't be rid of. Management were afraid of her and inclined to lead a quiet life, ignoring the daily upset she caused, in the hope she'd leave, or die, or worse! And they had to admit that she knew her stuff, was admirable in her administrative chores, assiduous in her every duty. None could fault her in-depth knowledge, historical memory and loyalty, for she carried out the job at hand with painstaking industry, to the credit of the company.

She was, you might say, very old school, set in her ways and old-fashioned ideas and wasn't one to modernise. She wasn't keen on much of I.T. and still did her work on an old typewriter, bashing away at every key with perfect grammar and impeccable spelling. Punctilious in every way, she was the very model of efficiency, despite her outmoded working methods.

Her dress, too, was somewhat dated, but it suited Miss King down to the ground. She had no wish for current fashions and the trend to dress so casually, preferring a smart skirt and jacket, the suit that was her uniform. It stood the test of time, she said. Her shoes were always nicely polished, heels mended and toes un-scuffed. It was worth paying more, she said, worth paying for quality.

# The Travelling Apple

Miss King was full of her airs and graces, with her affectations and superior ways. That's what her colleagues around her thought, as they watched her walk her corridors of power, back straight and head held high, a confident and purposeful step, homing in on her next victim. They heard the plummy voice ring out, in horror at a dirty mug left in the sink of the communal kitchen, half its contents left inside. Miss King herself used a cup and saucer, bone china with roses on. Each time used, she would wash it out, carefully and taking her time. No marks left around the rim, no stains hidden upon its base. Her colleagues laughed as they watched her go, washing up bowl and liquid in hand, fancy tea towel at the ready, Irish linen, properly ironed. No thrice-used mug for Miss King, they said, no swilling it out throughout the day. Miss King was the real McCoy, they said, Miss King was pukka stuff.

Miss King she was, Miss King she remained, for no one knew her other name. She didn't hold with first name terms and winced if anyone tried to discover it. It seemed to her so disrespectful, over-familiar and far too casual. It was up to her to raise the bar, to maintain the standards of yesteryear, but the directors didn't help in this and she was forced to plough a lonely furrow.

Nobody really knew Miss King, save for her haughty and disciplined ways, but the younger staff meant to find out. They wanted to know what her hobbies were, what she cooked for a meal at night, where she went on holiday.

Miss King, they knew, always worked late, intent on burning the midnight oil, clattering away on her old machine with a certain panache and wizardry. The carriage moving back and forth, in steady rhythm with her hands, the flawless script ever apparent, as she did her work with certainty.

They watched Miss King turn out the lights, pick up her bag and close the door. A large bag, it seemed to them, as they waited in silence at the end of the floor, discreetly hidden in the shadows. They followed Miss King from the premises, keeping a safe distance behind, occasionally having to run and catch up when she turned a corner and was out of sight.

On and on through the streets they went, wondering when she might take a bus, but Miss King carried on, her pursuers coming behind her unseen. Little did she know they were there or she'd never have carried on her way, would never have given them the chance to see what she really got up to every night.

Turning into a doorway then, Miss King suddenly vanished from view. The door was fairly nondescript, with nothing whatever to mark it out. You could easily have passed on by, so ordinary was the door itself. No number, name or letterbox, no sign to hint at what lay behind, no doorman or concierge stationed there.

The two friends gently pushed the door and found it opened onto steps. Several of them, going down, the light fading with each one, as they slowly descended into the dark. They appeared at the bottom to be faced with a wall, with no means of moving forward. The pair were considering what to do when the sound of voices broke the air. Two men hovered above them, wondering why their path was blocked. 'Is there something wrong with the switch?' one asked, pushing between them to see for himself. 'You *are* here for the girls?' he said, without waiting for any reply.

At the press of a switch, the wall slid open, revealing a large auditorium within. Dazzled by sudden light and music, the friends strained to see ahead, as the man who'd spoken pushed them in, the wall now closing swiftly behind them.

Round tables filled the room, all set out in cabaret style, in front of a stage with disco ball lights. Waiters moved with consummate ease, taking orders and bringing drinks, as the excited chatter of party guests increased in volume till it reached its crescendo.

The friends were ushered to a table, near the middle and piled with food. They sat and ordered a couple of drinks and waited for the show to start.

The lights were dimmed and the band struck up as a chorus line of girls appeared. There in the centre, outstanding amongst them, Mademoiselle du Roi, their own Miss King!

Now they knew what she had in that bag! Gone were the suit and the sensible shoes, replaced by stilettos and skimpy attire, the sequins catching the disco lights as she danced her way across the stage, undoubted star of the entire show. Gone was the plain and unadorned face, the pursed expression and crabby jowls. Instead, a well made-up visage, with glittery eyes and bright red lips. Nothing prim and proper here, though the look of concentration remained, as she danced her moves with practised precision.

Removed from her usual daily garb, she actually had a pleasing shape, a definite beauty with long slender legs and graceful arms that waved upon an imaginary breeze as she shimmied her way about the room.

The friends were stunned by what they saw, at the transformation there before them. Where was the office reptile now, the predatory brute that blighted their lives? Mlle du Roi was charm itself, full of poise as she worked the room. No stern countenance here but a happy, friendly and relaxed manner, at home in her sequins amidst the lights.

The friends had at first begun to snigger when they saw her name emblazoned in lights, flashed up onto a big screen. They laughed at the name she'd chosen for herself, a French translation more fit for the stage. Mlle du Roi was something else, for the erstwhile woman they knew as Miss King! They began to play around with the name, taking pleasure in alternatives: Mlle Bois de Boulogne and Mlle Eel de la Cité, a nod to the east end where their office was sat.

It was some time after the show began that the pretty *danseuse* recognised them. The look of horror on her face as she spotted her colleagues sitting there, was a sight that others wished they had seen. Twirling round upon the floor, she finished her dance in extraordinary haste, making her exit with an impressive flourish, vacating the stage for the rest of her troupe.

The friends stayed on till the end of the show, then left together the worse for wear, several cocktails having been consumed. They agreed to meet the following day to determine how best to spill the beans and let their other colleagues know. Should it be in front of Miss King or embarrass her behind her back?

The office floor was full of chatter the moment the friends arrived on the scene. Miss King, it appeared, had not arrived, her room as she'd left it the night before. It didn't take long for the rumours to start, for the gossip mongers to sow their seeds: Miss King was ill, Miss King was dead, Miss King had finally gone and retired.

But then the music started up and a door flew open in the entrance hall. Silhouetted in the light, Miss King in all her regal splendour, shimmering in satin of a violent blue, dancing her way across the floor, to the astonishment of those who witnessed her.

She danced with vigour for a full ten minutes before changing her stance and rounding on them. What were they doing, standing about, mugs of coffee in their hands?

Her voice bellowed like a lion's roar that shook the very ground beneath them. Colleagues scattered in all directions till every one was back at their desk. Service had been resumed again.

# A DEATH IS ANNOUNCED

Gerry was one of those people who read a paper from cover to cover. Assiduous in his reading, he went through it in its entirety, starting with the headline story and working his way through to the back page, right down to the small print. That he had the time to do this, was something in itself, *why* he should choose to do it was a matter for Gerry alone.

He particularly loved what he would call 'the interesting bits', the items that didn't always make the televised evening news, such as the list of famous birthdays and the daily court circular. But his favourite section of all was the column of obituaries.

He loved to read about people's lives, who they were, what they'd achieved. Not the so-called celebrities so much, but the ordinary man in the street. Often a shorter piece, a couple of sentences even (merely announcing the death), it made him wonder what the deceased would think and whether they were happy with the words in print. He decided, therefore, to write his own and, so that he could gauge the reaction, he quickly determined to send it off now. He'd place it in *The Times* no less and wait to see what happened.

On the day his item appeared, Gerry raced to the shop. Not to his local agent, as he didn't want to be seen. He'd hate to give the game away and reveal he was still alive. Better to sit at home and see if the phone would ring.

He sat and read his piece, chuckling to himself, for it sounded rather good:

*We are sorry to announce the long and painful death of Gerry McIntosh. Not peacefully and not in his bed but at the theatre, eating a box of chocolates. One, we now know – his favourite, strawberry truffle – had been infused with cyanide, by a person or persons unknown. He died eating what he loved and for that we must be grateful.*

Gerry waited in for three whole days before hearing any comments concerning his death. One or two people called at the house but left again when nobody answered. Condolence cards were dropped on the mat but with the usual banal platitudes, which only served to upset him greatly. Where were the grand outpourings of love, the wailing and weeping at the door? Where were the flowers and funerary wreaths, the heartfelt laments and affectionate words?

At the end of a week, he could stand it no more. Donning a very heavy disguise, Gerry marched off down the street. He sat in the cafe on his own, nursing a tea and a buttered crumpet.

Before too long, some women came in, one of them holding a copy of *The Times*. Their conversation sounded heated, with voices raised and angry tones. All talking over each other, it soon became apparent to him that few people believed him dead and thought it one of his practical jokes. All agreed it was in bad taste and that something really ought to be done.

Two days later, sitting at home, Gerry heard the delivery van. A parcel for him had just arrived, beautifully wrapped with ribbons and bows. Excitedly, he tore it open, but was surprised to find the gift inside: a large box of strawberry truffles. He took them to the theatre that night – which proved a fatal mistake.

# THE PORTRAIT

It was a Sunday on the edge of winter. Cold, dreary and raining, as days often were at that time of year. Short, in terms of the daylight hours, but long in terms of the utter boredom and utter loneliness that Tommy now felt since losing Freddie. She'd been, he thought, the love of his life, the one he'd been seeking since college days and had hoped to lead to the altar before long.

But Freddie had gone, upped and left him. Just like that, without a word of explanation and without any sign that she wanted out. Gone, without saying goodbye or leaving a note, but gone for good, out of his life and into another.

So here he stood, on a dark, wet afternoon, with countless others in a London gallery, dripping water over the floor as it ran off his clothes to form little puddles at his feet. He was soaked right through, from the torrents outside, as they fell from the heavens like a mighty river, overwhelming all in its path.

He'd run along the street from the station, collar turned up, hat pulled down, dodging the crowds as they bustled about, in threes and fours like miniature armies. Their umbrellas their weapons of choice, brandished about in unruly directions as they struggled to keep them straight in the wind, threatening to remove an eye or two and spear it on the lance-like point.

Once inside his favourite gallery, Tommy headed deep within, in the hope it might be warmer there, but shivering in his overcoat, he was forced to deposit it back at the door and start afresh in another room.

He moved about in a reverent silence, pausing at every hallowed piece before coming to rest at the focal point, his eyes drawn to the woman before him as she stared out to meet his gaze. A strong face with a determined look, a steely intent behind those eyes. Dark and resolute, constant and steady, astride a long, narrow nose above fixèd lips and all within an expanse of white – the lead powder that covered it all. At once recognisable, this Virgin Queen, with her red hair and striking looks, bedecked in jewels and regal finery.

Tommy wanted to kneel before her, in awe at her power and majesty; to pay homage to this formidable queen, as she kept him riveted to the ground before her, her eyes never leaving his face.

But who *was* this stately woman, this self-styled prince in a world of men? And was she really as here depicted? Tommy sat on a bench and stared, at the images surrounding this dignified queen. Tommy knew little of art history – Freddie had been the one for that – though he'd always been good with a canvas and brush. He'd set up an easel in their London flat and regularly stood with palette in hand, mixing colours and applying paint. Not very often portraits though, except the one he did of Freddie.

Portrait painters tended to flatter, to please the subject in front of them. Imagery was often used, to depict how the sitter wished to be seen and to manipulate their public image, both then and for posterity.

Here in front of him, Gloriana, projecting power from every pore, in her richly woven and sumptuous gown, triumphant at quelling the Spanish Armada. Nowhere could he see 'the body of a weak and feeble woman', hidden beneath swathes of material and virginal pearls, but the 'heart and stomach of a king. And a King of England too!', stamping her authority on the world stage as her hand rested upon a globe.

Did art imitate life, he wondered, or did life imitate art? Had anything changed since Tudor times or were we all just the same? Freddie, he remembered, was very particular when he took out his camera to take her picture. She thought that she had a 'best side' and wouldn't be photographed head on. Nor would it be with her hair unbrushed or striking anything but a feminine pose. When caught unawares, she was never happy and demanded the evidence be destroyed, like all those ghastly passport photos where she couldn't smile and couldn't pout. As a last resort, there was Photoshop, which proved that the camera often lied, similar to the portrait painter striving to achieve a favourable image.

Tommy had always assumed that role, seeing Freddie as she wanted to be seen, never seeing the person beneath. The image had always held fast, as Elizabeth's had for her many suitors, when presenting herself as a woman of beauty, with her high forehead and pale face. Even into her old age, she carefully chose to maintain this vision, to appear flawless and hide her scars – the pockmarks from a common illness. Freddie too was good at this, carefully crafting her external image, a mask to hide her proper face that she kept concealed from all who knew her. No one but Tommy knew the real Freddie and Tommy had chosen to ignore it.

Such had it been with the royal courtiers who toadied and flattered their primping queen, until such time as Lord Essex burst in, catching her plain and unadorned, without her wig and powdery shield.

Tommy had left it too late for this as Freddie had gone without a trace, showing her up for the coward she was. In truth, he'd known it all along but love is blind in refusing to see. He should have left her a long time ago when the cracks in her makeup began to appear, revealing the reality underneath. Even now, he wanted to turn away, to refuse to believe that the mask had slipped. But as he'd said to his brother once: 'When someone shows you their true colours, you shouldn't try painting a different picture'. It was time to put his easel away.

# RANTZ (WITH A Z)

Eight till six, they said, eight till six. In other words, the entire day, thought Mary, the entire day. Heaven help her, what would she do all day? She didn't like being inside to start with, but waiting for the plumber was about the giddy limit. It had to be done, there was no way round it, but why were there no two-hour slots, which would just about be manageable? A ten-hour window, for Heaven's sake, that was more than she could bear.

Mary stomped from room to room, wondering how to fill her time. She'd been up since seven, getting ready, checking the pipes under the sink, clearing enough space around them. And that was another problem, she thought – where was she going to put all this stuff? She really must sort it out some time, but not today when she was mad already. Back under the sink it would go, until the next time the plumber called.

Where, indeed, was he? Mary looked at her watch again. It was only ten past eight. Late already, in her book. Checking the time didn't help, it only made the wait seem longer. But what to do for ten hours, for she knew he'd undoubtedly come at six. She'd never been the lucky one, first on the day's list. Usually, she was last in the queue, almost like someone had planned it all. Put Mary last, they said, and give her something to do.

Last was Mary's middle name. Mary Last Jones. She may as well have been christened it, all those years ago. In fact, that was when it had all started, down at the baptismal font. She should have been christened on her own, like her elder siblings had been, but no, not Mary. That wasn't Mary's luck. She was there with five other babes, all being done at once, at a new communal service. And Mary Jones was last in the queue. Not only that but the priest was tired and had promptly dropped her in. A cardinal offence, surely, drowning a newborn babe in the font, much akin to other crimes like laughing at a funeral or letting go of the coffin. But no, he got away with it and the choir sang on.

Sixty years later, she was here at home, again surrounded by water. Her life slowly ebbed away as she waited for the plumber, towels all soaked like her christening gown had been.

Mary glanced at the clock. Half past eight. Thirty minutes gone and still no sign of him. She dared not go in the garden in case she missed his call, so pottered about indoors, looking for something to do. She stared out the window, checking for a van, but however long she looked, no van came.

It was just like waiting for the lift, down at the shopping

mall. It seemed to take an age and Mary had often resorted to hammering on the door in the hope it would speed it up. As the minutes ticked by, five and then ten, she would hammer louder still as she watched her food defrost.

Why did nothing work in this technological age? The lights were often out and the buttons wouldn't press; the doors would open and close of their own free will; and the lift smelled of pee from those who couldn't wait.

The shops themselves also bothered her, with their badly spelled signs and their ever-moving stock. Just when she knew where the cucumbers were, they'd put them somewhere else, in a spot she'd never guess. Other salad items remained where they were, but not the cucumbers, no, they were lying with the fruit.

How many hours were wasted there, if she totted them up over the course of the year? She couldn't claim those hours back, that time had already been lost. The only one to benefit was the shop owner himself. For while searching in the aisles, by the carrots and the leeks, she had often picked up food that wasn't on her list. That, of course, was the plan, of the cunning marketing folk, but Mary wasn't impressed as she spent too much.

What she *didn't* buy (and knew she never would), were the ubiquitous hot cross buns, sold all year round. It was only a matter of time before they sat with the Christmas puddings. Mary just despaired at the commercial side of it. Every day blended into one, with nothing left to look forward to. The spirit of Christmas she had known as a child, was now shoved aside for financial gain, with cards in the shops before spring was over. This year, she had seen them in May, in order to catch the tourist trade. Before too long, the tinsel would be up and we'd all be sent into a frenzy again.

Music would sound from every shop, with Noddy Holder belting it out, suggesting we hang our stockings up. Mary had nothing against Noddy – or the rest of the band for that matter –but she did wish he would learn to spell. She itched to correct him every time she saw the title of some of his songs, written on party playlists: 'Cum on Feel the Noize', she read, and then 'Skweeze Me, Pleeze Me'. What sort of an example was that, to the younger generation?

Perhaps she was an old stick in the mud, but she was a former teacher too, and longed to get out her old red pen and strike a line through it all. She could see where it all headed already, with Christmas commonly spelled with a cross. Say 'x' to 'Xmas' she said and give it its proper name.

The world had truly gone mad, she thought, with too much slang creeping in. Informal ways of spelling words or trying to abbreviate them ('tonite' and '2nite' were prime examples), should never really have been allowed, not according to Mary Last Jones.

So much seemed to have changed, in just twenty years or so. Another one of Mary's gripes was the amount of noise everywhere. What was wrong with the sound of silence, Mary dearly wanted to know. You couldn't go and buy a dress without loud music blaring out – and never the music she liked. She'd hate to be a sales assistant, having to listen to that all day.

On trains, she sat in the quiet carriage, though even that was now abused. It used to be a haven of peace, somewhere she could read her book, but now it was treated like an office, with work calls and business chats. Mary would tut and start to shush but it never seemed to have effect and the guilty parties carried on.

The theatre wasn't much better these days, not since they turned it into a bar. At one time, it was sacrosanct, with no food or drink allowed, unless during the interval. This had changed like everything else and the crackling sound of a plastic cup as someone took their last sip, was just too much for Mary to bear. That and the opening of a bag of crisps, that invariably shattered everywhere. And don't get her started on mobile phones, even when in silent mode. Not only distracting for the audience, with their bright screens flashing on, but dreadful for the actors on stage when a ghostly face lit up the room.

It was like they couldn't do without, constantly looking and checking in, as if their life depended on it. You'd see them walking down the street, phone in one hand, coffee in the other. The two essentials of modern-day life.

And that, thought Mary, was another thing. The

constant need for food and drink. If she looked at the shops in the average street, or at those on her overground station concourse, all she could see were eateries, of one wretched kind or another.

And then there was the smell of them, especially when taken on the bus! She'd seen a whole manner of food, or smelled it, which was more to the point! Hot porridge, jellied eels, oven pork ribs in a barbecue sauce. The bus just wasn't the place for this, though nobody else seemed to mind.

Mary's stomach started to rumble, despite the thought of the mobile food. She glanced at her watch yet again but this time found that the hands had moved and were edging towards twelve o'clock. Still no sign of the water man, Mr Aquarius as he came to be known.

She rustled up a bowl of soup, home-made yesterday, then wandered back to the other room after checking the state of her kitchen floor. Please God, the man would come soon, as she was fast running out of towels.

Mary looked out into the street and shook her head despondently. A growing forest of wheelie bins, blue, black, green and brown, spreading as far as the eye could see, encroaching on every path and drive. She hated it when they were put out early, two days ahead occasionally, for it spoilt the look of the avenue.

Worse than that, Mary could see, was the mess where the dog owners hadn't picked up. Not all were inconsiderate,

Mary knew that well enough. Most, in fact, were very good and carried it home in those little bags, though it wasn't something that *she* could do. Others seemed to taunt her with it, hanging a bag upon a tree or dangling it from a nearby rail, as if to decorate the street. Little Fido might be lovely, but oh that he could look after himself when his owners plain refused to do it.

Still no sign of the plumber man, still no sign of a white van. It could, of course, be a different colour, emblazoned with large lettering, but no van had come this way and no one had rung to say they were coming.

Just as she sat herself down at the table, Mary heard a loud thud. She rose to see a delivery van, moving off at quite a speed. This might be the books she'd ordered and she raced to the front door to see. As usual, he'd thrown them over the fence, narrowly missing a row of plants. Why on earth had the man not knocked? Her new books might be damaged now.

The clock hands shambled on, until they reached six o'clock. For ten hours, she'd sat here, ten hours biding her time, as Mary Jones had known she would. Last in the queue yet again. What on earth did it take to be first or even to be met halfway?

At length, the bell finally rung and Mr Aquarius was standing there. 'Evening, love', he jauntily said, brushing past her at the door. Mary Jones bit her tongue and ushered him into the wet kitchen.

'How are you?' she just about managed. 'Have you had a busy day?'

'I'm good', the young man said, which made Mary want to scream. Another phrase from America, another phrase that she'd come to hate. What was wrong with 'I'm fine', Mary really wanted to know. What did he mean by 'I'm good'? Didn't that mean that he wasn't naughty?

At least he appeared to know his job, as he busied about under the sink. Everything seemed to be going well until he broke an old pipe. Water surged in all directions, soaking them both from head to toe. He rummaged in his bag for tools, then said he'd need to go to his van.

Mary watched as he drove away and knew she'd have to start again.

# LETTING GO

Cynthia watched as another balloon floated up into the sky. They always advised not to do it these days, for the terrible harm it was known they would cause, but people still did – and regularly. Up and up the balloon went, higher and higher, a speck of light caught by a midsummer sun on a late balmy evening in June.

Sky lanterns they called them, as if it would make a difference, as if it would lessen the damage inflicted on some poor unsuspecting creature, for whom ingesting them meant near-certain death.

Widely witnessed and documented, they were still released into the air, in celebration at happy events or to commemorate a loved one. But what goes up must come down, in one piece or in tiny fragments, often with fatal consequences.

It was not a scene one wanted to witness, the slow and painful death of a bird or a sea creature entangled in string. Cynthia had seen it when walking with Ken and had never wanted to see it again. Ken, her marine biologist husband, taken from her in the course of his work just nine months ago. She'd always known that his job could be dangerous but had never thought it would come to this. She'd put that side to the back of her mind, as any sensible person would do, allowing him just to get on with the job.

She watched another balloon go up and wondered who it was for. What was the story behind this one and who had it let go? Who might it be in memory of and who had they left behind? Would another death be a consequence and would they ever know? Perhaps it had been for a happy event, though the outcome would be the same.

Her mind wandered back to her childhood and the joy of a red balloon. All balloons were good in those days – red, yellow, blue and green – but red was her favourite colour. She never could blow them up, she just didn't have the puff. She would try and try till her cheeks were sore and the balloon was full of spit. Then she would hand them to her dad, who was left to finish the job. He never seemed to mind at all, as long as his girl was happy.

One of her friends had been scared of balloons, like Cynthia was frightened of spiders. It was said that one had burst in her face, at a children's birthday party. Bits of balloon lay everywhere, just like the sky lanterns did. And then there were those deflated balloons that looked like a razor strop, limply hanging from every door and corner of the room. Unwanted by any child.

But Cynthia thought of happier times and playing with her dad on the beach. She remembered the huge sandcastles he made, proper ones with moats. Then later as the tide came in, they'd watch their defences breached. Across the beach they'd run together and jump into their boat, made of sand by her clever dad, who would captain them both ashore.

Her dad was no longer with her now, having died many years ago. She remembered the pain of letting him go but willing him back again. In her mind, she watched him on their boat, sailing over the sea. She fancied she saw, on a distant shore, others awaiting him, and the further he drew away from her, the closer he moved to them.

Her eyes were never misty for long when she thought of the fun they'd had. Flying her kite up on the heath, her father teaching her how. 'Don't let go!' he had always said. 'And watch for the drag and the lift.' Cynthia clung as tight as she could, to the strings of her simple kite. She loved to watch its diamond shape dancing in the sky, rising and dipping on gusts of wind, to the sound of her own delight. One day, of course, she did let go, when a downdraught startled her. The kite was wrenched from her tender hands, causing some blood to flow. How Cynthia had cried that day, at the loss of her diamond kite.

Her parents had bought her a bicycle, in a bid to cheer her up. Something new to entertain, in her favourite colour, red. She'd never had a bike before and was somewhat in awe of it. Sitting proud upon the saddle, holding the handlebars, she felt she'd be ready to take on the world if ever she learnt to ride.

Her father taught her the rudiments and showed her what to do. He'd been a cyclist all his life; it was how he'd met his wife. Peddling down the lane one day, he'd skidded on black ice. He ended up in the hospital with a fractured pelvis and ribs. Pat was the nurse who attended him, destined to become his bride.

Within a year of marrying, Cynthia appeared on the scene. A pretty girl with curly hair and a little button nose. The apple of her father's eye, the one he loved the most, even more than his only son who followed two years on.

Her brother already had a bike when Cynthia was given hers. He'd shown an interest early on and had first been bought a trike. Quickly learning to master that, with a boyish derring-do, he'd pestered his dad for a bicycle – but it was mum who'd given in.

Cynthia always admired him, her active younger brother. On his bike he had an ability that she at first would lack. He had great balance and confidence, right from the word go, whereas Cynthia needed stabilisers and her father's steady hand. 'Don't let go! Don't let go!' she often used to cry, but her father finally did just that, to let his daughter fly.

How proud he would have been of her, in the annual cycle race, hurtling past the winning post with mud upon her face. For time itself had now flown by, since Cynthia was a girl. Orphaned, married, widowed, alone, was how she described herself. She still went out on her bike every day, all through the countryside. She loved the feel of the wind on her face and the freshness of the air, the flat of the pedals beneath her feet and the turn of the bicycle wheels. Exhilaration filled her mind and the fibres of her body, as she reached the top of every hill, then freewheeled down again.

Back at home, she would settle down with toast and a cup of tea, before turning again to the task at hand, whatever that task might be.

It was nine long months since Ken had died and probate had just come through. Now she felt she must sort out the house and look at her life again.

She remembered the scene at her parents' house, when her father had passed away. Her mother was very practical in donating all his clothes. 'It's only a pile of shirts', she'd said, 'not the man himself', but Cynthia had found it all a struggle and far too emotional. She could picture her father wearing them and had quietly held some back. Even now, when she came across them, pushed to the depths of her cupboard, she would bring them forth and cling to them, as if her dad was there. They'd lost his scent after all these years and she was all the sadder for that. She'd always found it comforting, to have a little sniff, to hold those shirts against her face, find solace in their touch.

Her dad might even have laughed at her, for keeping his clothes so long. 'You're cluttering up your house', he'd say, 'it's time to let them go'. She knew there was some sense in that and he wasn't teasing her, just trying – as ever – to encourage her and assist her in moving on.

She remembered finding a box of balloons, beneath her father's hats. Twenty or thirty, brightly coloured and waiting for a party. She took two from the little box, her favourite colour, red, but still she couldn't blow them up and sneaked a laugh at that.

Now here she was, centuries on, or so it felt to her, preparing to go through this all again, as she looked at her husband's gear. Tracking equipment and radios that she'd certainly never use, cameras, binoculars, hydrophones, beakers, nets and tubes. She didn't know what half of it was and had no thought to learn, for Cynthia had a fear of water and couldn't even swim. Ken was going to teach her once but she'd kicked up quite a fuss. God hadn't made her with flippers, she'd said, she'd been built for dry land.

Cynthia rummaged through the cupboards and piled up his diving suits. They took up quite a chunk of room and she'd be glad to be rid of them. She'd also be pleased to be shot of the smell, of the sea and rotting fish. She should never have let him keep them indoors, with their algae and bits of kelp. That was love, she'd come to decide, a lot of give and take. After all, he'd put up with her bicycle, as it stood there in the hall.

In the weeks to come, she made many trips, to the charity shops and the dump. She was certain that Ken would approve of this, of her new and determined stance. 'Take the emotion out of it', she was sure she could hear him say, just like her mum when her dad had died, though she'd found it impossible then.

Cynthia worried she was acting too fast, as if in nine months she'd forgotten Ken. But that wasn't the truth at all and she carried him in her heart. She'd always been a sensitive one, from a very early age, but now had to try and shake it off, if she were ever to carry on. In her ear, she heard her mum again, talking about possessions. 'They're not your man, they're only *things*', her mother would surely say.

Perhaps she would just keep one or two, that wouldn't take up space. As long as they weren't marine related, she chuckled to herself. She picked up a trophy that Ken had won, for scuba diving techniques. That would be the next to go, she decided doggedly.

Sitting down to take a rest, she pondered the way ahead. Scanning the room and a line of books, there was one that caught her eye. She didn't recall having seen it before, so it must be one of Ken's: a book about Chinese philosophy and the writer Lao Tzu. The Tao, a particular way of life, was one that Ken had admired. She'd often hear him speak of it and the lessons of the universe.

The book fell open as she picked it up and she gazed at it in surprise. A sentence that could have been written for her had boldly been underlined:

# The Travelling Apple

'New beginnings are often disguised as painful endings', she read. Cynthia looked out into the hall. It was time to take out her bike again.

# BRANDY FOR THE PARSON

Cold. Dark. Two am. No sound, save for the anxious breathing of the men and the oars combing the water. Five in the boat tonight, four rowing and one with his hand on the rudder, helping to guide them in to the shore. Their movements were barely perceptible as they inched ahead, steadying their course. All in the boat were hushed. It was always the same. The fear and anticipation. The worry they'd be seen. But it was black out there, the moon barely visible as it ducked behind the clouds that threatened a storm. The sea was like a millpond as yet and for that they were grateful as they rowed inland.

It was their fourth mission tonight, a small taste of success, mixed in with the salt upon their lips and the spray from the stroke of the oars. But the night was far from over and there wasn't a single man amongst them who was ready for revelling yet.

Quick, furtive glances from one to another, were the only communication they allowed themselves in this well-rehearsed routine. Each man knew the job in hand and none would veer from the course. They knew the dangers only too well and wouldn't place a comrade at risk.

The prow cut through the water as the boat neared the shore. The men held their blades as the waves rolled them gently in, like someone unfurling a carpet. The landing was now upon them.

Waiting under the cover of darkness, villagers dressed in sombre clothes, ready to move as the boat came in. The usual signal, like the hoot of an owl, told them the cargo had just arrived. Wading into the water's edge, they hauled the boat upon the shore, as those aboard jumped quickly out.

Scenes of frenzied activity followed, in contrast with the earlier calm, as boxes were passed from one to another and kegs were rolled upon the sand. They worked to get the booty off, to start the run to their hiding place. Each man working as a team, each with his own regular task, knowing what he had to do, for if one failed then they all failed and that was never an option.

The *Lady Caroline* had gone aground, as many a ship had floundered before her. The word had gone out that her hold was full, rich pickings for those who dwelt near the sea, however illegal and dangerous to steal. Its sailors had to be dealt with first, always a bloody operation, if the precious horde was going to be seized. That accomplished, it was all hands on deck to transport the cargo from ship to shore.

Tonight the stash was great indeed: tea and tobacco, brandy and lace, silk and wool and barrels of gin. Something for every villager there and without the need to pay any tax. Material secreted on their person, in deep pockets and the lining of coats; the heavier spoils hauled away on strong men's backs and with the help of a horse.

Up the hill from the beach they went, avoiding the usual turnpike road and the paths where the guard were likely to be. Across the fields and amongst the sheep, the line of smugglers made its way, each of them bearing forbidden treasure, carried with care and undisguised love. A convoy of clandestine contraband on this well-trodden and even track. Each one walking behind the other in reverent silence and contemplation.

By and by they entered the village and onto familiar and hardened roads. The clattering of the horses' hooves awakened the hamlet from its quiet slumber, though little stirred as they entered in. The sound of softly running steps ensured that curtains were all kept closed, as everyone knew what the footsteps meant in the early hours before the dawn. Mothers kept their children sleeping, closing their eyes to the morn's events. They'd learn the trade themselves soon enough and join the fathers of the village whenever a ship did run aground.

On to the church the smugglers went, where the parson stood awaiting them. He turned a blind eye to the marauding men, keen instead to view them as foragers, supplying his poor and needy flock. He wasn't averse to helping himself, though in truth the spoils were readily given, for the kindly use of his underground vaults. Some would say he was aiding and abetting but the parson looked out for impoverished folk, applauding the men who furnished them and saved them from real and barbaric starvation.

Enjoying a sup from a previous raid, the parson gladly opened the door, letting them down to the storehouse below. Removing the flags from the stone floor, the kegs were deftly transferred down, to waiting hands and willing hearts, along with the chests of tea and tobacco, the boxes of silk and foreign lace. The floor was carefully sealed again, no trace of the disturbance occurring there.

In the churchyard outside, more business took place as the stone lids of the coffins were raised, empty save for the dirt and the dust and the cobwebbed corners of the spiders' trade. Smaller tubs were placed therein or hidden in the village pond, for collection at a later date when none were likely to be seen or caught.

In this close-knit community, the goods and the men were safe tonight, the horses slept within their stable and the womenfolk could breathe again. No need for pistols, cudgels or clubs, no hangings upon the turnpike road. The mission had been an unholy success and the parson could drink to their health again.

# THE BRIDES OF MARCH

Olive and Mary were friends. They'd been friends all their life. Born within a day of each other, they lay in adjacent cots, destined to be that close throughout their entire life. There they lay, little legs kicking, wide-eyed with wonder and desperate to start their adventures together. Even at that age, they seemed to work in unison, giggling together and crying together. The midwife had joked that they even filled their nappies at the same time! Double trouble, she'd said, and she wasn't far wrong. It was like they'd made a pact, as soon as they saw each other, a knowing look in those baby blue eyes and something of a hint of mischief.

Their parents had never met before then, not even at the ante-natal class. They'd been in the same room but had never actually spoken, there having been a baby boom and a hall full of anxious parents. Yet, somehow, across that crowded room, the babies-to-be had united, simultaneously stirring and making their presence known.

The mums having finally met, they too formed a bond and were soon ringing each other up, swapping stories and seeking advice. They began to meet on a regular basis, either for coffee in each other's homes or pushing their prams around the park, to the admiring coos of other women.

As the girls began to crawl, it seemed that they were joined at the hip. Their movements were totally synchronised, as if hours of training had been put in. It was mesmerising to watch the pair, moving in the same direction and always at the same pace. Never a step out of place but completely aligned, as though stuck with glue. The rhythm of one matched the other, as they stopped, then carried on their way, oblivious to those who were watching them. They seemed to know instinctively exactly what the other was doing and moved as one with utter precision.

The trend continued as the girls grew older. They were instantly recognisable as they walked down the street on their way to school, right foot then left, swinging their arms in the usual perfect symmetry. No one could tell the girls apart as they strolled along in their uniforms, hair tied back in a ponytail. It was only if they were met head on, that anyone could tell the difference, though even then it was quite uncanny as they shared the same expressions and features. It was just as well they had different names or they really would have merged into one.

They followed the same path at school, choosing the same subjects to study and excelling with identical grades. Offers from university matched and the pair didn't deviate from their choice, opting to go together to Cambridge, a stone's throw from their family homes.

Olive and Mary hailed from March, a pretty Fenland market town on the banks of the River Nene. Once an island in the middle of marshes, it was lately used by pleasure boats. It was also known as the starting point for the annual thirty-mile walk to Cambridge, by students and academics alike, notably in the month of March. Olive and Mary had joined in the walk, singing with gusto as they went, enjoying each other's company.

The two girls loved the Fens, the low-lying land so rich and fertile. They loved to explore, on foot or by bike, or by taking the occasional narrowboat, cruising along the waterways at a sedate and leisurely pace. Passing through The Great Level, they looked for flowers and wildlife, spotting the warblers and dragonflies and awaiting the arrival of swallows in spring. If lucky, they might sight a deer, standing still in the marshland or crossing the water in search of food. Scanning the banks, they looked for voles, piles of nibbled grass a sign and burrows at the water's edge. Ratty, of *Wind in the Willows* fame, who loved to mess about in boats. Their dearest wish was to see an otter, but they'd need to be there at a different time, at dusk or dawn, to catch him out.

Looming up ahead of them, dramatic above the flat landscape, the Ship of the Fens, Ely Cathedral, sailing towards them on a sea of green. Little did they know it then, that they were each destined to marry there, as brides of two men of the church, sons of one of the cathedral staff.

On through life went Olive and Mary, girls no more but pretty young women. They graduated with first-class honours, celebrating together in style and looking resplendent in their college gowns. The champagne flowed like the River Cam, along which they travelled by punt, lying back at the stern of the boat as the 'pusher' drove the vessel along. How handsome he looked, standing there, his muscular arms pushing the pole, then letting it drag behind the boat as they gently glided along the river.

At the journey's end he helped them out, introducing himself as Charlie Hicks, brother of Andrew, chorister. He asked if they'd come to evensong, in the college chapel, the following night, to which they agreed readily.

As the sun was setting on another day, the women sat in a pew near the front, listening to the psalms and canticles. A sense of peace surrounded them, as the music carried them heavenwards, reaching into their very souls with its angelic air and celestial beauty.

The women were truly swept away, by the music yes, but also the brothers. Charlie had sat with them in the pew, as they listened to Andrew's singing prowess, whispering to them occasionally, to explain the traditions of evensong and its origins in the Catholic Church. Andrew's voice was simply divine as he stood there composed, with his music sheet, plaintively singing the *Nunc Dimittis*. How wonderful to be able to sing, to stir the emotions and ease the heart.

Charlie and Andrew were very attentive when they took the women to dinner that night. They dined on hake in a green sauce, accompanied by a crisp dry white and lively and roguish conversation. The evening ended with a walk by the Cam, along The Backs towards Jesus Green. A goodnight kiss on a sultry night, to seal their new relationships.

In the coming months, the romances blossomed and the four regularly went out together, Olive and Andrew, Mary and Charlie. The women were always inseparable and one wouldn't go without the other, to the mild amusement of their new beaux. At times though, they found it a little frustrating, as they thought it might hamper their relationships, but in time they accepted them as they were and managed instead to laugh it off.

The women, on graduating, had remained in Cambridge, sharing a house near Grantchester. Both had found jobs locally, Olive at the Fitzwilliam Museum, Mary at the botanical garden. Neither were jobs that either one wanted but it was a step in the right direction and both would look good on their new CVs. They wanted, of course, to work together and plotted how they might manage that.

Charlie and Andrew were older than them, both studying for a PhD. The two were in their final year, one very much a classicist, the other a criminologist. They knew not where their work would take them, but knew that they wanted the girls in their lives, and so, before the summer was over, both men had gone down on one knee and proposed that they marry the following year. The date was set for 15th March, not the most auspicious time, given its links with misfortune and doom, a fact not lost on Charlie Hicks with his knowledge of Roman history. It signalled, however, the end of term in the academic calendar, and a date when Ely Cathedral was free.

Olive and Mary began to prepare, putting together their wedding list and sending out their invitations. They enlisted a friend to make their dresses and regularly went for fittings together. The women were nothing if not consistent, not only choosing the same material but also choosing the same style. Peas in a pod they'd always been and peas in a pod they'd remain. Charlie and Andrew laughed at this, till they spotted themselves in a mirror. Both were dressed in morning suits – black herringbone and tailcoats – with ivory waistcoats underneath. They certainly knew how to cut a dash, their slender frames rendering them stately. Many a female head was turned but the men had eyes for no one else except their beloved Olive and Mary.

The months flew by and the day approached. The excitement in the female camp was lately reaching fever pitch, mothers of the brides-to-be selecting their outfits and wedding hats. Broad-brimmed or fascinators, which would be the ladies' choice, as they raced together from shop to shop? They had to ensure they wouldn't clash or steal the show from their beautiful girls, on this, their very special day – and in such a fine cathedral no less!

The end of February came around and Charlie had got the jitters. Some put it down to pre-wedding nerves but his brother knew this was different. The omens, Charlie said, were there, from the change in the weather to the birds in the sky, from the way that the wind moved through the Fens to the cracks appearing in the cathedral roof. They really ought to postpone, he said, for it wasn't worth taking the risk, by inviting the worst upon themselves.

The brothers went for a walk together, trying to decide what ought to be done. Should they tell their brides of their fears and chance not finding another date, or should they go ahead as planned and keep the omens to themselves? The pair engaged in much debate as they wandered through their college grounds, discussing the many pros and cons. They walked by The Backs, from Jesus Lock, and along as far as the Mill Pond. At length, they opted to go ahead but not without some trepidation.

The day itself soon came around and Charlie was in a terrible state. He seriously wanted to cancel the event on this, the Ides of March. The night before, he'd had a dream, that foretold of the brides' demise. They really shouldn't be going ahead, but how to tell the girls?

The hours ticked by and the brothers set out, dressed in their morning suits. The cathedral held an eerie silence as they started off down the nave. Anxious faces greeted them instead of the expected smiles and waves. It was clear that the brothers hadn't heard what the rest of the congregation knew. There'd been a terrible tragedy and their brides had both been killed. Leaving home in their bridal boat, their punt had overturned. Neither Olive nor Mary could swim and the two had quickly drowned. The upturned boat was testament to the women's untimely end. Their two bouquets upon the water, in sad and silent tribute.

The brothers faced each other in horror as the dream became too real. Over and over in Charlie's mind, it kept revealing its ugly self, reminding him it had been foretold that the women would meet their end.

The organ played a funeral march as the guests filed through the doors. Charlie and Andrew led the procession, walking with slow and heavy steps, sorrow etched upon the faces of these empty, lonely men. They looked to the river with tear-stained eyes for the women who never came. Together in death as they'd been in life, the sad brides of March.

# TAKE COURAGE

Characters:

      Workman

      Drover

      Brewer

      Horse

Scene:

A deserted street on the Isle of Dogs. It is early morning. In the distance, the clatter of a horse's hooves and the rumble of a cart. A man is on his way to work, dressed in old jeans and a checked shirt. He turns as the noise becomes louder and a brewer's dray rounds the corner.

Man – Whoa there!

(The horse and cart bear down on him.)

Man – Whoa there! Stop!

(The drayman is slumped on top of the cart, his hands still on the horse's reins.)

Man – Whoa! Whoa!

(The man stands in the horse's path, waving his arms up and down, trying to make himself look bigger.)

# The Travelling Apple

Man – Whoa, boy! Steady! Steady!

(The horse stops right in front of him with a loud squeal while the drayman topples further to one side.)

Man – Hello! Hello there!

(The horse snorts air out from its nostrils, its head jerking up and down.)

Man – (To the drayman) You there! Hey! You there!

(He approaches the drayman and grabs him roughly by the arm, but quickly has to stop him from falling off the cart.)

Man – What the …!

(He sees the drayman is drunk and can't sit up.)

Man – (To the horse, stroking his long face with his palm.) All-right, all-right, ea-sy, ea-sy.

(The man lets out a small whistle in exasperation.)

Man – Hello there! Anybody about?

(The street is silent, save for the horse occasionally scraping a hoof on the ground and giving another snort.)

Man – (To the horse) Easy boy, easy.

(The man checks that the carter is safe and not in danger of falling further off the wagon, then takes the horse's reins. He makes a clicking sound with his teeth, to get the horse moving.)

Man - (To the horse) Come on boy, let's get you home.

(The man leads the horse away along the street, pulling the cart behind him with the drayman asleep on top.)

Man - (Continually talking to the horse.) Easy boy, easy.

(The slow and gentle sound of the horse's hooves and the

wheels of the cart clattering along behind is all that is heard for some time, until they reach the brewery.)

Man – (To the horse) Home now boy. Well done lad.

Man – (To the brewer, appearing in the yard) He's yours now. Over to you.

(The man pats the horse's neck with affection, turns and walks away.)

# WRITER'S BLOCK

Ricky looked at the blank sheet. He'd sat here all morning and had written nothing. Not even a sentence that had been scratched out. He couldn't remember a time like this, not since his school days and the end of year exams. He vividly recalled looking round the hall, watching his classmates scribbling away, nineteen to the dozen. From the fire of the gun at 9 am till the whistle blew at 12 o'clock, their pens just raced across the page while he sat staring into space, unable to write a word.

'Have a glass of sherry first', one of the teachers had jokingly said, 'it will help the creative juices flow'. But Ricky's pen was lacking ink and Ricky's mind was lacking ideas. He'd watched his friends beavering away, wondering how their thoughts arose and if they wanted to share them out. Ricky's exam head was simply empty and he stared blankly into a void. The more he stared, the worse it became, as he sat gazing round the room at the feverish hands wielding a pen. He'd done his revision diligently, but someone, it seemed, had siphoned it out, leaving a hole where data had been. What a waste, all those hours at night, toiling away to then forget, each scrap of knowledge torn to shreds, each piece of information lost.

He heard the pens upon the page, filling up a dozen sheets with words of wisdom and the deepest thoughts. He watched as his friends hunched over desks, inspiration driving them on, to higher marks than he'd achieve with a vacant mind and an empty page.

There was nothing that Ricky could possibly do but sit and wait for the ordeal to end. The invigilators watched him closely, expecting a burst of activity, so Ricky tried to look deep in thought and hoped he'd find a sprint to the end.

No such sprint or surge occurred, not even a stumble or small step forth. Ricky Walsh was entrenched in his furrow, waiting for the sound of the all-clear.

He failed his exams, unlike everyone else, a surprise to those who knew him well. For Ricky was very intelligent and normally placed at the top of the class. Something had happened in those few days, that had wiped his mind of all that he'd learnt. He was forced to take the exams again and the following year excelled in them.

Thirty years on, he was struggling again, this time in his new career. He'd spent some years in publishing, editing other people's work, but now he was keen to write his own and try to make his name as an author.

Ricky was very widely read, devouring the written word before him. There was nothing he wouldn't stop to read, be it cereal packet or roadside hoarding. His literary tastes ranged far and wide, in several different languages, fact and fiction, poetry and prose. He enjoyed a variety of different genres, both classics and contemporary. He could always be seen with his head in a book, turning the pages avidly.

His shelves were crammed with every author, arranged in height where space allowed and sorted into different sections to enable him to find his favourites. A pile of books in every corner, stacked and waiting to be read, bought at fleas and in charity shops. He always read a book to the end, however painful it could be, believing he owed the author that, after months and sometimes years of work.

Those he enjoyed he always kept, slotting them into their place on the shelves or lying them flat across the top if the existing stock couldn't squeeze them in. He'd always find a space for them; it just required a bit of thought and shuffling round of the other books. He loved to sit and admire them, running his eye across the spines, checking they lived with their families, though some had found an adopted space. Every so often, a lone being was stranded in a place of its own, waiting to find its soulmate and be paired for life with its newfound friend. What a joy to match these books, sit them together side by side, in happy union forevermore.

Ricky's house was full of books, with shelving units in every room. There was even a little row in the toilet –

paperbacks on the windowsill. Not that he ever read while in there, it was just a handy space for more.

He looked forward to buying a new shelf, to house what he hoped would be his own work. He may even have it specially made, for when he had published his first book. How exciting that would be, his name on the spine for all to see! He'd give it pride of place, of course, and keep it free from dust or dirt.

But that was still a long way off, as Ricky hadn't published yet. In fact, he was only a few chapters in and had now come to a crushing halt. He had no idea where his story was going, who was involved or how it would end.

Ricky looked at the blank sheet. He'd sat here all morning and had written nothing. Not even a sentence that had been scratched out. He'd never been lost for words before, not when entering competitions or writing reports in his various jobs. The words had simply flown from his pen as the contents spilled from his active mind. Perhaps he should try that glass of sherry to start the creative juices flowing. But Ricky sadly had none in the house and a cup of tea didn't feel the same.

He moved from his chair and walked round the room, running his hand along his books in the hope they'd impart some magic fix. But they chose instead to keep their secrets and left him out of their sacred circle.

Sitting down, he looked once more at the plain sheet in front of him. A virgin page if ever there was, untouched and infertile. If only something would come to him, a little spark to set him alight, a little flash of genius. Instead, he sat in a total gloom, the only light from a blank white page.

Up he stood and moved to the window, to see what was going on outside. The birds were singing in the trees, never at a loss for words, their speech fluent and capable. Even the dog next door had voice, articulate and meaningful, as he made himself known to the neighbourhood. Oh that Ricky could find such words, arrange them on his empty sheet. Bald and unadorned it looked, as it met his gaze with its pleading eyes, begging him to be inspired. But inspiration had packed its bags, upped and left in a moonlight flit, leaving Ricky quite bereft.

Down he sat at his desk again, fingers drumming on the page while his mind remained quite vacuous. He knew it must be full of thoughts but what would drag them from their lair? Restless as the day wore on, frustration creeping through his veins, Ricky put his pad away, hoping to give his head a break. He'd lost direction with his book and needed to find his way again. If only there was a handy map, if only the path was clear.

He tossed and turned in bed that night, covers on, covers off. Was this how other writers lived, in a constant state of flux and turmoil? Did they too have sleepless nights or did they lie in sweet repose? He kept a notepad by his bed, just in case some thoughts occurred, but that too remained untouched as he turned the pillow yet again.

Finally drifting into sleep, exhaustion then consuming him, he dreamt of a library full of books, his name on every one of them.

He woke with a start at 10 am, three hours later than his usual time. The sounds of the world outside flooded in as he opened the window to let in some air. Into the shower Ricky went, allowing the cold water to flow over him, in the hope it would waken his every sense and jumpstart his brain into action. He felt less flat as he breakfasted, on high-protein eggs that energised and a very large mug of black coffee. He hoped they would make him more alert and provide a mental stimulus.

Back at his desk, they had no effect and the page before him looked stark again. His head was in need of a thorough spring clean, so he took himself out on a country walk. Along the lanes he walked and walked, over green fields and over the stiles, up the hills and down again, through the woods and along by the stream. He breathed in air that was clean and fresh, watched as a vole crossed his path and listened to the sound of a woodpecker, drilling away on a nearby tree. He felt the cobwebs blow away as a gentle breeze tickled his neck and he heard his notepad calling him from the other side of the clapper bridge.

Crossing over the granite slabs, Ricky suddenly quickened his step. Storylines were in his head and he began to know how his work would flow. His characters all mingled about, begging him to return to his book and let them live upon the page. His mind was suddenly full of chatter, of anxious voices calling him, urging him to hurry along, lest he forget their messages.

Ricky stood upon the step, fumbling in his coat for keys. Panic rising with every move, he checked his pockets time and again, but all they yielded was a handful of coins, a chip fork and a betting pen. Ricky, it seemed, had locked himself out. The door was closing on his characters too, as his head was filled with the missing keys and what he could have done with them. And then he remembered his sister's advice, to hide some keys in the garden troughs, in case the door should shut behind him. But which one had he placed them in and had he even remembered at all?

Ricky rummaged in the soil, his nails clogging with wet earth. His fingers surprised a large red slug, lineolated with outstretched tentacles. The slug quickly drew those in, sensing a predator in its midst, though Ricky was just as scared of him! In a wavelike motion, the slug moved on, leaving a trail of slime behind him. It seemed he'd been the guardian of the keys, for there beneath the layer of mucus, the objects that Ricky was looking for.

Back inside the house he went and headed straight to his chaste white page. How welcoming it seemed to him now, inviting him to feel its surface and looking forward to his gentle touch.

The words now flowed on the sheet before him like a river having burst its banks. He could scarcely write quickly enough as the ideas came flooding out, covering up page after page. Ricky loved to feel his pen, gliding along like a skater on ice, never stumbling, never falling, but passing over the stretch with ease.

Ricky worked late into the night, his brain on fire with new ideas. Barely a word or sentence crossed out, he carried on till his mind was spent. His efforts had clearly worn him out and he flopped into his bed that night, content with all the progress made. The story's end was now in sight and tomorrow he hoped to finish it.

The Muses came in force that night, hovering over Ricky's bed, whispering thoughts and inspiring him. They gave him the power to finish his book and when he'd written the final word, he dedicated his work to them.

Soon the book was on his shelf, his name adorning the cover and spine. He began to ponder a second book and thought he'd call it *Writer's Block*.

# THE OVAL SQUARE

It was a Thursday morning in mid-October. A weekday just like any other. The sun hadn't yet come up and there was a hint of autumn in the air. The leaves on the trees had started to turn and were beginning to show their seasonal colours of red and gold. A noticeable chill greeted the day but one that felt good and very welcome after a summer of unbearable heat that had stretched its legs into the final quarter.

Nicky was on her way to work, glad that the back of the week had been broken. The last three days hadn't been good, stuck at her desk writing reports, with too many deadlines nearly missed. Her job had become overwhelming with too many chiefs placing demands and never being appreciative. There were not enough staff in the office these days and no hope of employing more as cuts in funding continued to bite. Every day seemed the same, a relentless plod on an interminable wheel that creaked with the effort of moving on. Starting early, leaving late, she never had time to catch her breath and the effects were starting to show.

People were always offering her seats, even the elderly and pregnant women. She felt bad at accepting them, but knew she'd collapse on the spot if she didn't and so readily slumped into the welcome space. Her eyelids drooped and her shoulders hunched as she willed herself to stay awake. This was on her way *in*; she was ten times worse on the journey home.

Sitting on the bus that morning, Nicky leant against the glass, propped up like a tailor's dummy. Barely conscious of the world outside, she drifted into a deep sleep. In no time at all she started to dream. Images came and images went, shapeless and dancing about like jelly, refusing to be identified, never settling but moving on. Voices echoed in her brain, indistinct as if under water, the odd word caught on a wave.

The lurch of the bus forced her awake but only for a moment or two as she fell back into a reverie. Lulled in and out, as though on a tide, she found herself at the terminus, a gentle hand calling her. At first struggling to come to, Nicky suddenly sat up straight, looking around in bewilderment. She'd missed her stop by several miles and would now be forced to travel back and arrive at her desk an hour late.

The hand now coaxed her from her seat, guiding her to leave the bus, like someone helping the blind to walk. A simple 'thank you' was all she could muster, as she moved unsteadily down the road, half awake and half asleep.

The man who had helped her, caught her up and offered the use of his cricket bat to shore her up while she gained some strength. She might later see the funny side, as he stood there in his cricket whites, but for now she felt as if still in a dream. Boarding the bus that would take her back, Nicky gave the man a wave, then settled down on the front seat.

Fighting to keep her eyes open, she started to doze off again. She was vaguely aware of the other passengers, coming and going and shifting seats and the driver's call to move down the bus. Their voices mingled with the sounds outside and the monotonous speaker announcing the stops. 'Town Centre', 'Pine Grove', names she was all too familiar with, from her daily commute to and from work.

A new and unexpected name suddenly brought her back to life, making her question if the route had changed. 'Oval Square,' the speaker proclaimed. 'Next stop, Oval Square'. It sounded so matter of fact, not like something just made up or the fabric of her dreamlike state. Yet the name itself didn't seem real, just didn't seem that concrete.

It all sounded very odd, just like her day so far had been. First of all she had missed her stop, then she had met a cricketer. Nicky had never liked sport in her life!

She finally arrived at the office, to raised eyebrows and knowing looks. She was the first at her desk, every day, and invariably the last to leave, but here she was, behind them all and not a word to indicate why. Some of her colleagues exchanged glances, noting the bags beneath her eyes, while others carried on with their work, typing away furiously.

Nicky's day was the same as ever, attending meetings, preparing reports, with never a moment to scratch her leg.

She managed to grab a cup of coffee en route to meet her new boss, but only because *he* wanted one. Lunch was again out of the question. She'd become very used to the daily hunger and eating very late at night. That was the way it was.

The journey home was uneventful and she caught the bus as she always did. 'Town Centre', 'Pine Grove', 'Royal Oak', 'Green Park'. The latter she found unimaginative and wondered why it had been so called. Someone couldn't be bothered, she thought, when tasked with giving the park a name. But at least it described it well enough, with its swathes of lawn and acres of trees. You could hardly call it 'Grey Park', unless tarmacked over and without any flowers.

The next stop was 'Oval Square' and Nicky sat up at the mention of it. How could a square be oval she thought, for an oval couldn't be square. Imagine the poor chicken if it laid a square-shaped egg! Nicky felt bound to investigate when next she had a day off.

It was something of a conundrum, she thought, as she continued to journey home. Why it should matter, she couldn't say, but it occupied her thoughts. For a start, she'd never heard the name, on her usual daily commute. But twice she had heard it voiced today, so assumed it must be new. The whole concept puzzled her though, as it dizzied in her brain. What was a square, after all, or any other shape? Did they have to stay the same or could they assume another form?

Square pegs and round holes, square people and square meals, began to bother her. None of them now made any sense and were at once ridiculous. Angular images frightened her as they gathered en masse in her head, marching towards her, square-bashing, in a persistent and angry drill.

And then she heard the leather on willow, in a corner of her mind. She turned and saw him bending there, ready again at the crease. She waved but he didn't seem to see her and the bus carried on.

Nicky was glad to be home that night and flopped in her easy chair. Her head was now all over the place from her day at work and the square. All manner of shapes persisted now, but the square was still at the front. Nothing could shake it from her mind, so she opted to go to bed. But she hadn't eaten and couldn't sleep and the image appeared again. It seemed to dance in front of her, mocking and teasing her, now a plane, now a cube and then the oval square. Why was this image haunting her? What did it want of her?

Two days later, a Saturday, and Nicky had had a lie-in. She'd been kept awake most of the night, oppressed by the oval square. She resolved to go on the bus ride and look for the Square herself. She wondered when it had come into being, when it had been devised. For she did this journey every day and to her it was quite unknown.

What would the Square be like, she thought, and was it

a square at all? Was it a village or market square and would it be square or oval? A square was a square was a square was a square, so Nicky had always thought; four sides equal in length, a geometric in every sense. And yet the idea hammered away that a figure could change its shape. Take, for example, a boxing ring, not round but typically square!

Perhaps no form followed a pattern and did what it wanted to do. She had once heard of a square near Hastings, comprised of only three sides. Its fourth 'side' contained no buildings but was open to the sea.

The Oval Square might also deceive, if ever she came to find it. Nicky considered what its aspect might be. If shaped like an egg, in two-dimensional form, it would have no sides, straight edges or corners, and be totally closed at the top and the bottom. What sort of a square was that? And was it an oval, an ovoid or ellipse?

Nicky's mind went off at a tangent, seeing that all was not as it seemed. She'd never been fond of disguise or illusion and kept her feet in the real world. She'd never enjoyed a magic show or watching a woman get sawn in two by someone performing a conjuring trick. She knew that this was all deception and couldn't see the point of it.

Back on the bus she journeyed along, listening out for her stop to be called. But somehow she found she had missed it again, as she ended up back at the terminus. Thinking her mind had been distracted, by shapes, forms and nonsenses, Nicky took another bus back and waited for the announcements again. She remembered roughly where it was, somewhere after 'Green Park'.

But 'Green Park' came and went and still 'Oval Square' wasn't called. Nicky decided to get off the bus and ask for directions from passers-by. As nobody seemed to have heard of it, she walked and walked around neighbouring streets. Frustration growing with every step, she sat on a bench to think. Where was the elusive Oval Square, for it couldn't have run away!

It was then that she caught the sound again, of leather hitting willow. A cheer went up from a distant crowd as someone yelled 'Owzat?' Training her eyes across the park, she saw a figure move. She fancied it was the man in whites and determined to go and see. Perhaps he would know of the Oval Square and tell her where it was. But as she walked across the park, he seemed to disappear. By the time she'd reached the other side, there was nobody there at all. Only a pair of cricket pads, propped against a tree.

Stumped at what seemed like a ghoulish trick or deceitful sorcery, Nicky decided to go back home and end all this mockery. She'd had enough of squares and cricket, of shifting shapes and the like, and wanted to return to normality, back in her cosy home.

'A parcel was delivered for you', a card in her mailbox said. But looking in the usual place, there was nothing there at all. I'm sick of these games, Nicky thought, as she put the key in the lock.

She sat down to a cup of tea and a slice of Madeira cake. Then her eye was suddenly drawn to her lawn and a cricket ball. Something flat was under it and Nicky went out to see. Crudely drawn, in a childlike hand, a map of the Oval Square.

# MRS SANDY

We don't know a lot about Mrs Sandy. Almost nothing actually. In some ways, she was an invention although she was in fact very real. Not just in someone's head but an actual person, living and breathing and walking her dog. A golden retriever. Or was it a labrador? Either way, the dog was the colour of sand. Hence its owner's name. Mrs Sandy.

No one knew her real name. She was always Mrs Sandy, so called by my maternal grandmother who watched her go by every day from the window of her ground-floor flat. Regular as clockwork. Well, you have to be, don't you, if you've got a dog. They need their walks and to do their business and the owners like to go with them. These days they are seen jauntily carrying those little bags to pick up their dog's mess but back in Mrs Sandy's day – somewhere in the 1960s – niceties like that were not so common, ruining the stitching on many a good shoe of many a good person. Mrs Sandy of course may have been more modern, more kindly to her fellow pedestrian and may indeed have picked up after her dog. She was just never seen, as far as we know.

# The Travelling Apple

We don't know a lot about Mrs Sandy. Not her height, not her dress, her bearing or her age. All we know for certain is that she was Mrs Sandy, owner of a sandy coloured dog. There were other such people along the street but none that were given a name. Mere passers-by, en route to work, off to the shops. Invisible in their identities, as such Mrs Sandy would have been if it weren't for her dog. As such the dog itself would have been if it weren't for Mrs Sandy! Two unremarkable beings, probably joined at the hip, as owners and their dogs often tend to be, each with an identity given it by the other (albeit unknown to themselves) and passed on through my grandmother, who gave them an immortality simply by seeing them pass before her window.

We know the character of neither, dog nor Mrs Sandy, or whether there was an extended family. Yet every day they walked along the street together, side by side in quiet communion, seen by a lady elderly and housebound for whom the daily walk gave daily pleasure. Perhaps that is why she immortalised them, gave them their own family name to be preserved for posterity, made them into friends of her own, on the other side of the glass, without ever having the chance to speak to them or pass the time of day.

I never knew Mrs Sandy. Never saw her, never spoke to her, but she's always been real, always a part of my life since I was a little girl. Mrs Sandy and her dog, who maybe never knew they'd been seen and who never would have guessed they'd be part of my family history.

Mrs Sandy and her dog. They should make a statue of them.

# THE HOLIDAY

Ellie could tell easily which of those in the queue it would be. Just by looking at them. It was the same every time. As if they were wearing a sandwich board announcing it to the world. 'It's me', it would say, 'I'm the one'. But she could tell that, without the advertisement. There was just something about them. Their looks, their gestures, their posture, the way they treated their husbands. If only she could put them all on a beach together and let them fight it out. Or on a coach.

She wondered why she put herself through this and yet here she was again, partner in tow, eyeing up those who she knew would cause problems. It was usually the women, sometimes the men – but only when stirred into action by their dominant womenfolk.

Laurence couldn't see why it really mattered and had often suggested that Ellie just ignore them, but how could she, when they were so blatant every time?

Laurence and Ellie were off on holiday. They'd chosen Andalucía this year, as recommended by Brian and Sue, their next-door neighbours with the teenage boys. One of them, Stu, was learning Spanish and was hoping to go to university next year. As a family they had been to Spain, to let him practise his language skills, though in truth he'd ended up speaking English as it all seemed so much easier.

Laurence and Ellie had booked their trip and were very much looking forward to it. Advised not to go in the summer months, when the temperatures reached over forty degrees, they'd opted to go in late spring, when the climate would be more favourable to those unused to the searing heat.

And now here they were, at Gatwick Airport, lining up to go through Security. She'd already seen them, jumping the queue and rushing from one side to another, trying to move a step ahead. It was just like in the supermarket, where they planted their husbands in a neighbouring queue, to see who reached the checkout first, then switched sides at the last minute, to the consternation of those around them. Tutting didn't cut any ice. They seemed to be immune to it.

Ellie soon lost sight of them as she and Laurence browsed in the shops. So many perfumes on display, all at the usual eye-watering price and all blending into one, as testers were sprayed on arms and wrists. They looked at clothes and sunglasses, at canvas bags and money belts, at biscuits, sweets and bottles of wine, but didn't choose to buy anything. Ellie was very organised and had planned their holiday weeks ago, purchasing all they could possibly need for their eight days in the south of Spain.

After a coffee and early lunch, at the usual hiked-up airport costs, they made their way to the departure lounge. A number of people were there already, claiming the seats by the check-in desk, with the intention of being the first to board. Ellie looked at Laurence and sighed, not sure whether to laugh or cry. Some were already forming a queue, doubly determined to stake their place and get ahead of the rest of the pack.

Down the ramp to the transit bus, pushing and shoving and gathering speed, as if the plane were about to depart. Ellie wanted to trip them up but didn't want the flight delayed, so continued quietly on her way, aware there'd be other times for that.

Her first victory came on the bus, as she and Laurence knew it would. Last on, first off, in prime position for boarding the plane. She didn't attempt to suppress a laugh as the earlier competitors were all held back as she took her time in finding her seat. Right by the emergency exit, with extra room for Laurence's legs.

Finally, they were all sat down, lockers closed and seatbelts fastened. All in their allotted seats that they'd fought so dirty to secure.

Before too long the plane was off, a direct flight to Málaga. As soon as the seatbelt sign went off, the passengers were up and down, opening lockers, looking for bags. Some fiddled with the air control while others called for the stewardess. Down the aisle the trolley came, stopping and starting like a car that had stalled, as some who already needed the loo squeezed past in a sideways move, disturbing those in adjoining seats.

Ellie sat and watched them all as the toilet queue stretched down the plane. There were more in line than in their seats, or so it seemed to her just then. As they swerved and swayed in their holiday clothes, they resembled a colourful Chinese dragon, dancing along to the plane's rhythm. But fire would breathe from flared nostrils when later they heard the pilot announce that everyone must return to their place as the cabin crew prepared for descent.

Off to claim their baggage next, amidst the usual worried looks that either it hadn't arrived at all or someone else had taken it. Then on into the arrivals hall and a nervous scan of the waiting crowd as they tried to locate their tour guide.

Mónica Paz awaited them, gushing and effusive in her general welcome as she ushered them all to the waiting coach, grinning madly from ear to ear. Mónica had not allocated seats, believing this to be too draconian, a decision she would come to regret and one of her many rookie mistakes. For as soon as the door of the coach was opened, there came the sound of a roaring stampede as her passengers fought to gain entry and reserve for themselves their favoured seats. One had even taken hers and was already testing her microphone! Mónica looked at the scene around her, a carnage of suitcases left on the path, as their owners settled themselves in.

It was much the same when they reached the hotel, as a human wave washed from the coach, all determined to check in first and go and grab a jug of *sangría*. Last off were Ellie and Laurence, all good manners and graciousness, calmly taking their place in the queue and acting like nothing unsavoury had happened.

The following morning breakfast strode in, with all eyes on a slow toaster. Mr Muffin stood on guard, directed by his wife on sentry duty. She was certain their bread had gone in first, whatever Mrs Beak might say, and would stand here firm until it popped out, her husband providing the backup team.

On the other side of the room, meanwhile, a contretemps was taking place between one of the guests and the hotel waiter. Mrs Eye for the Main Chance was there, standing her ground on the bread rolls, maintaining the six were her husband's breakfast. The waiter had seen her filling them all and wrapping them up in some serviettes. Not just those but some hard-boiled eggs and sundry pieces of fresh fruit. Then she'd taken some bottles of water and put them in her capacious bag, undoubtedly brought for this overt mission.

Ellie and Laurence watched in horror as the woman unashamedly left the room, taking her lunchtime goodies with her and leaving the waiter open-mouthed. He'd already, in fact, lost the battle, as countless others were doing the same and there wasn't much point in claiming it back. He couldn't exactly recycle it.

Onto the coach and the usual scrum, with six competing for the front seats. 'You can take it in turns', the tour guide said, as if addressing a bus full of kids, but her words were all drowned out in the fray, till Mrs Pushy took first prize and the coach settled down again. Useful to carry that parasol, Mrs Pushy smugly thought, as she casually folded it back in its case.

The group was heading for the Picasso Museum, though not everyone was pleased about that. Some were real enthusiasts while others' displeasure showed on their face as they misunderstood the artist's work. A breakaway group started to form despite the pleas of Mónica Paz, who was keen to keep them all together. She could only watch in some despair as she saw the renegades start to escape the minute they alighted from the coach. The rest of the party, the obedient, followed Mónica into the museum and happily spent two hours there.

Rounding up the deserter pack, an hour late it has to be said, Mónica herded them back on the bus and off they went to the *alcazaba*, to admire the Moorish architecture and the beautiful jacaranda trees. Ellie noticed a pop-up picnic going on in the welcome shade – Mrs Eye for the Main Chance, handing her husband his hard-boiled eggs.

The afternoon was spent in the grounds or wandering round the old town, till they all met up as a group again to visit the city's impressive cathedral, built on the site of a former mosque. Mónica Paz sat and prayed that her group would all behave themselves, that tomorrow would bring a fresh dawn and see them doing what she told them to do. But her fervent prayers were to go unanswered, as God, it seemed, was out for the day.

Nor was He there the following morning as they left the hotel at an early hour, to catch the fast train to Sevilla. Bleary-eyed and half asleep, a ragbag of holidaymakers shuffled along untidily, looking like war-torn refugees but without any hope or will to succeed. An early breakfast had been arranged, though few were up in time for that, having spent too long in the hotel bar, quaffing wine and tasting sherry.

Bright-eyed and bushy-tailed, Ellie chatted to Mónica Paz, who felt she'd found a friend at last. Ellie could be an ally, she thought, should anything start to go wrong today. She'd seen the way she looked at the others and felt she'd be a kindred spirit, helping the day to run more smoothly. She and her nice partner, Laurence, who always seemed so interested and attentive to all that she had to relay.

First, they visited the tobacco factory where Carmen had worked with other women, rolling cigars between her thighs. Passionate and sensual, her own woman and full of fire, she would easily have been more than a match for the troublesome ones in Mónica's group, who were already making lewd remarks as to where the cigars would have ended up.

On from there to the Plaza de España, a very grand, semi-circular square around which were alcoves with benches, one for every province of Spain and decorated in colourful tiles. Ellie and Laurence hired a boat and drifted along the square's canal while others strolled around the park in which the square was situated.

Lunch was in the Jewish Quarter, on a *tapas* crawl in its tangle of streets. The group were left to their own devices, as Mónica couldn't bear the strain of moving them all from bar to bar and helping them order their *raciones*. She did explain the system to them and suggested a few favourite treats before letting them loose to fend for themselves, to come back hungry or satisfied.

Mrs Eye for the Main Chance bemoaned the fact that she hadn't had time to pack her own lunch, as breakfast had been so early that day, but her grumbles were carried away on the air and thrown into the Guadalquivir.

Re-grouping after lunch (and a quiet nap on a bench for some), Mónica led them round the cathedral, its immensity surprising them all. She took them out to the patio of orange trees, the courtyard of the former mosque where Muslims had once performed their ablutions before entering this holy place.

Inside, she pointed out Columbus' tomb and guided them round the most noteworthy chapels, before leading them all back out again to what was once the minaret. While some braved the climb to the top – by a series of ramps instead of steps – others complained that it had no lift and wouldn't be worth it anyway.

Back on the train to Málaga, the group chatted about their trip. Ellie was keen to show them her photos, particularly those from the minaret, which revealed the most spectacular views!

The following day was free time and many were found by the hotel pool. Their towels had gone out before six o'clock, as Ellie and Laurence had known that they would, and there they remained the entire day, even when no one was using them. The satisfaction that Ellie gained was seen later on in the restaurant where the lobsters she saw were not on her plate. Nursing some raw and tender burns and barely able to move with the pain, they knew they would have to cover up, as they couldn't risk that sun again.

They left Málaga the following morning, travelling by coach to Córdoba, where they'd spend the next couple of days. In the evening, they attended a flamenco show at one of the best local *tablaos*. Mrs Pushy and her entourage fought their way to the front seats, though this only served to backfire on them when the dark-haired woman in the polka dots invited them up to dance on the stage.

Not one to be trifled with, she hauled the women up before her, showing them the expressions to use, the pride, posture and flirtatious moves. Arms gyrating and feet stomping, the women were a frightful sight as they struggled to follow anything, from the swish of the skirts to the footwork and yells. At least they received a round of applause, from sheer politeness and courtesy.

The women all sufficiently recovered from what they saw as a grim ordeal, to enjoy the delights lined up for them in one of Spain's most beautiful cities. At first disappointed by its thick stone walls and stark exterior resembling a fortress, they – like others – were mesmerised when they stepped inside the stunning *Mezquita*. Row upon row of two-tier arches, in red brick and white stone, stretched as far as the eye could see, in this truly inspiring and astonishing mosque.

Walking through the forest of columns (850 if they counted them all), it was hard not to marvel at the beauty therein, a UNESCO World Heritage Site. And then they came upon the cathedral, nestling beside the more famous mosque, with its high gothic ceiling and Renaissance nave.

On from there to the bell tower, which most this time decided to climb for the views it afforded from the top. Some would be less impressed at night, with the bells of the city preventing sleep, but for now they were all hypnotised by the heavenly sights unfolding before them. Courtyards and patios full of flowers, whitewashed houses and wrought-iron gates, small squares and narrow streets beckoned them all as if calling to prayer.

The last leg of the tour approached as they left Córdoba en route for Granada, the final stronghold of Moorish rule, which fell to the (later named) Catholic Kings after eight centuries of dominance.

The Colonel, as he'd come to be known, was the first

one off the bus again, his wife having claimed the front seats by throwing her parasol onto them, narrowly missing someone's head. Dressed in his usual flannels and jacket, far too hot for the southern climate, he stopped to reprimand Mónica Paz about the quality of air on board the coach.

Mónica looked to Ellie and Laurence in the hope that they would help her out in shutting down this odious man. Ellie immediately came to her aid, looking the Colonel straight in the eye and telling him that the air was better the further down you went in the coach. Whether this was true or not, no one fortunately ever questioned, and the Colonel and Mrs Pushy were moved, to the silent applause of all on board.

How quiet it was when they next set forth, without the rush for the front seats and without the flight of the parasol. It almost seemed civilised with everyone sitting still in their place, though a low grumble could be heard near the back as the Colonel fiddled with the air controls.

The Alhambra topped the list that day and there was much discussion by those in the know as to why it wasn't a bingo palace. Two elderly sisters were quite disappointed to learn that they wouldn't be given cards or have the chance to win a prize. They'd hoped to hear the call in Spanish and had learnt the numbers one to ten, though how they'd have managed with sixty-six was something their tour guide could only surmise.

Much of the history was lost on them, as Mónica Paz did her best to run them through its residents, from the Nasrid sultans to the Catholic Kings and the later Napoleonic troops. Completely at sea with the dates and names, some of the group wandered off, while others hung on her every word, Ellie and Laurence foremost amongst them. This was to prove very important as they moved around the palace and gardens, the different areas making more sense than if, like others, they were facing them blind.

The tilework they found astonishing, with its colourful geometric designs alongside inscriptions and poetry, prayers and sayings in Arabic. It was hard to take in so much beauty, unveiled by a subtle and delicate light that filtered through from the patios outside.

Water, promoting a sense of calm, gently flowed from fountains and rills, its tranquil sound rippling over them as they made their way through courtyards and gardens, each one a paradise.

Ellie and Laurence sat in the shade, looking out at the houses below and the Sacromonte opposite. Their holiday now was slipping away and soon it would seem like a faraway dream. Before that, there was shopping to do, a few souvenirs and, for Brian and Sue, a special gift for suggesting this trip.

The group set forth the following morning for a couple of hours in the local shops. Tiles and pottery were popular, reminiscent of so many places they'd been. Some of them bought leatherwork – handbags for the ladies, belts for the men.

Their goods safely stored inside the coach, the party boarded yet again, for a ride around the surrounding plains. From there to García Lorca's house in the nearby Huerta de San Vicente. The house was almost exactly the same as when Lorca had sat there writing his plays. Killed far too young, at the height of his powers, it was poignant to think what might have been, had he not been shot by Nationalist forces at the start of the Spanish Civil War.

Poet, playwright, theatre director, an accomplished musician and artist too, Lorca foretold his own death, signalling his body would never be found. To date, said Mónica, it never had.

At five o'clock in the afternoon, the now emotionally worn-out group left the house in a fragile state. They returned to the hotel to start their packing and prepare themselves for their homeward flight.

It was a motley crew that arrived at the airport, some still wearing their holiday clothes, others ready for English rain. Subdued and now quite orderly, they quietly filed onto the plane, each taking their turn in the queue as if someone had sprinkled magic dust.

They'd left Mónica Paz in peace, waving a friendly *adiós*, vowing to return another year and set her some challenges yet again. But Mónica wouldn't be there for that, having hung up her jacket and tour guide notes. She'd accepted a job in the firm's back office, where she'd never deal with people again.

# The Travelling Apple

The journey home was uneventful and most of the group stayed sat in their seats, save for those with a weak bladder and those who tried to go anyway.

Ellie and Laurence raised a toast to what had been a remarkable week. *¡Viva España!* they both cried out, chinking their glasses and drinking champagne. Perhaps next year they would go again, hire a car and tour around. Or maybe they'd join another group and visit the towns they had not yet seen.

The decision was later made for them as they caught sight of a parasol, broken in two in a nearby bin.

# THE TRAVELLING APPLE

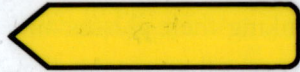

There it was again. Sitting right in front of her, round, red and healthy. Just like she'd seen it before. Several times.

Sas was on a journey to France, visiting old friends from her teaching days. She'd decided to take the train, as it was much more relaxing than going by air and all that waiting and hassle at the airport. She'd boarded the Eurostar in London, taking only a weekend case and a day bag for her lunch and book.

She'd made the sandwiches early that morning (ham and a bit of mustard), with some lettuce leaves on the side, more for decoration than anything as they'd probably wilt as she left the house. She'd also grabbed a packet of crisps (salt and vinegar, a long-time favourite), a chocolate bar (Milky Way), a bag of sweets and some bottled water. She could buy coffee on the train and any other food she needed, on the long journey down to Marseille.

Nestling at the bottom of her bag, quite forgotten amidst other delights, a Cox's apple, firm and fresh, taken from her fruit bowl at the last minute. She always put an apple in, never an orange (too messy), never a pear (didn't like).

# The Travelling Apple

A sort of companion for the trip, for the apple itself was never eaten.

Sas started her lunch as the train set off. Early for some, it could be said, but Sas had been up since six o'clock. Although she'd had a slice of toast, she already felt the hunger pangs and so quickly opened her sandwich box. The lettuce looked the worse for wear, though she ate the leaves all the same, as the woman in front was watching her. The mustard on her ham was hot, a trigger for a coughing fit and the woman to look for another seat.

Sas opened her book and read. Some short stories, by her favourite author, perfect for going on a journey, perfect for any time at all. She could dip in and out, just as she pleased, enjoying each of the tales in turn, rather than having to wade through a novel, forgetting the plot if she didn't keep up.

Two stories in, she put the book down, thinking she might now need a coffee. As the trolley hadn't appeared on the scene, Sas made her way to the buffet car. She bought a latte and a Chelsea bun, which she quickly consumed when back in her seat. She hadn't meant to eat it so fast, but hey-ho, it was gone now. She could always buy another.

Sas settled into another story, a tale about an oval square and a disappearing cricketer. The ball was a bit like the apple she'd brought, though she hoped the latter was not as hard. Crunchy, yes, hard, no, and definitely not soft. Sas hated soft apples.

She rummaged in the bag for her fruit and put it on the table before her. Just to remember the apple was there. She wouldn't want to arrive in Marseille and still have it in her bag. Best to put it where her eye could see it.

Not that that mattered a jot, as Sas had travelled here before. So had the apple, as it happened, though not the same one of course. Goodness, that would be disgusting! Think of the state it would then be in!

She often wondered why she brought it, as she knew in her heart she would never eat it. Not when there were crisps to be had. Or chocolate. Or Chelsea buns. But brought it she had, so she'd better eat it. After her Milky Way, that was.

She thought of when she went to Scotland. She took an apple with her then. And when she went to Wales. And Ireland. And Spain. Everywhere really. It had been with her more than her husband had and didn't complain as much. The ideal companion for her – one that liked to travel and one that didn't moan.

Sas delved into her bag again, shifting the apple on the table to allow more room for her bag of crisps. Her elbow caught the edge of it and sent it crashing to the floor where a passer-by nearly tripped on it, spilling the coffee in his hand. She picked it up and dusted it off, popping it back inside her bag, thinking she'd have to wash it now before she sank her teeth in it.

Sas continued to read her book, occasionally looking out of the window, trying to catch the names of the towns as the train rocketed through the stations. She had to change on reaching Paris, but Sas was more than used to that, having made this journey several times.

Reaching Marseille later that day, Sas met up with her teaching friends, joining them for an evening meal. *Tarte aux pommes*, a dessert too far, was looking up from its pastry case, challenging Sas with its apple slices, arranged in overlapping circles. She eyed it up for a moment or two before telling her friends she'd wait till later as she still had an apple in her bag. They laughed, as there didn't seem much contest, but Sas was adamant in her choice and steadfastly waited till back at the hotel.

She took the apple from her bag, noticing a little bruise, undoubtedly from its fall that day. She felt a tinge of sadness then, and guilt that she'd knocked it to the floor, causing it to hurt itself. Sas wiped the dirt from its tender skin, caressing it like a newborn babe, then washed it under the tap in the sink as if she were holding it over a font. Drying it off with a clean tissue, she placed it on the bedside table, admiring its fine, orange-red colour. There it sat, till she came to pack, after a hectic and fun weekend with her friends.

Guilt consumed her yet again, as she felt that she'd left it on its own, after its harrowing journey down through France. All alone, in the hotel room, it had loyally sat awaiting her, in the dark, without its friend.

Wrapping it up in some serviettes, Sas took care that it wasn't damaged, placing it at the top of her bag and making sure it wouldn't be crushed. She made her way to the railway station, peeking from time to time in her bag to check that her apple was still okay.

Once on the train, Sas settled in, her weekend having gone in a flash. She could hardly believe she was on her way home, as it felt like she'd only just arrived. She smiled at the man opposite, starting on his lunch already, a rather tasty-looking baguette filled with what looked like camembert. Sas was glad he was eating it now, as it might start to smell later on and give off a somewhat unpleasant pong. She noticed he also had an apple, which sat on the table in front of them, sad and lonely as her own had been.

She looked again inside her bag and gave her apple a little pat. She'd leave it where it was for now and let it just enjoy the ride, to avoid another calamity. She made her way to the buffet car, buying a coffee and two cheese toasties, readily consumed when back in her seat. The man had eaten his large baguette but the Golden Delicious had gone untouched. He'd propped it up beside his book, to stop it rolling back and forth, but every so often it teetered about, with the movement of the speeding train.

When London St Pancras was later announced, the man put the apple inside his bag. Sas quickly checked on the status of hers and found that all was calm and well. On reaching home, she took it out, swaddled still in its serviettes, and placed it on the kitchen counter. She wondered now what to do with it, as she'd feel like a cannibal eating it. There it stayed for a couple of days, while Sas decided what to do.

Eventually, she had an idea. She cut the little apple up, eating the parts that were not too soft and placing the pips on a fresh serviette. She waited until they had all dried out, then buried them in some damp moss, in a small bag in the refrigerator.

Six weeks later, she took them out and planted them in a nice green pot, specially bought for the little seeds. In truth, Sas wasn't expecting much and thought that they wouldn't germinate but, by and by, a shoot appeared, rising above the rim of the pot.

In the months to come, she nurtured it, moving it from sun to shade, re-potting as it started to grow. She gave her little tree a name, in memory of their trip to France. Apple Jacques was her pride and joy and stood there proud on her patio. It may not ever bear fruit, it may not experience gravity or the fame that Newton's apple had, but Sas' tree was very special, for the travelling apple had hung up its stalk and rooted itself in fertile ground, giving its owner a companion for life.

Vida Cody was born and grew up in south east London.
She graduated from the University of Southampton with
a degree in Spanish and went on to gain a Masters in
Hispanic Studies from the University of London.
She has lived and worked in Spain and Peru and
has travelled widely for both pleasure and business.
Introduced to books at a very early age, Vida has had
a strong love of literature ever since. *The Travelling Apple*
is her third collection of stories.